FIRSTBORN

FIRSTBORN

*f*IRSTBORN

ROBIN LEE HATCHER

TYNDALE HOUSE PUBLISHERS, INC.,
WHEATON, ILLINOIS

Visit Tyndale's exciting Web site at www.tyndale.com

Edited by Traci L. DePree

Designed by Jenny Swanson

Scripture quotations are taken from the *Holy Bible*, New Living Translation, copyright © 1996. Used by permission of Tyndale House Publishers, Inc., Wheaton, Illinois 60189. All rights reserved.

Library of Congress Cataloging-in-Publication Data

Hatcher, Robin Lee.
  Firstborn / Robin Lee Hatcher.
    p. cm.
  ISBN 0-8423-4010-6 (hc)—ISBN 0-8423-5557-X (sc)
    1. Illegitimate children—Fiction.   2. Teenage pregnancy—Fiction.   3. Adopted children—Fiction
  4. Birthparents—Fiction. I. Title.
  PS3558.A73574 F57 2002
  813'.54—dc21
                                      2002006065

Printed in the United States of America

07 06 05 04 03
9 8 7 6 5 4 3 2 1

To Jerry—
Because the Lord God said,
"It is not good for the man to be alone.
I will make a companion who will help him."
And He brought me to you.
R.

The birth of this book seemed to take forever, and it had more than one midwife to help it arrive safely.

First, I want to acknowledge Rebekah Nesbitt, who held my hand a lot. What a pleasure it is to work with you. Thanks for an abundance of patience.

Second, I say thanks to some very special women who met in my home for Saturday morning Bible study during the months I worked on this book. Lawanda, Josie, Barb, Evy, Sara, Ruth, Karen, and Muriel—your prayers were answered!

$\mathcal{P}$ROLOGUE

$\mathcal{A}$UGUST 1979

The late afternoon sun glared down upon the floating dock, baking the wooden plank surface and the three sunscreen-slathered teenagers who lay upon it, their feet dangling in the water. For the moment, the three of them were alone in the small inlet, the speedboat having taken another run up the length of the reservoir, pulling skiers in its wake.

Opening her eyes, Erika James glanced at the brown hills that surrounded Lucky Peak Reservoir, noting how little time was left before the sun would slip beyond them. Maybe a couple of hours at most.

She wasn't ready for the day to end.

She wasn't ready for the summer to end.

But she couldn't stop either of those things from happening any more than she could stop her boyfriend, Steven Welby, from leaving Boise tomorrow, headed for his first year at the University of Oregon in Eugene.

Her sixteen-year-old heart was breaking. No, it had already broken. She wanted to curl up and die.

She rolled her head to the right to look at Steven. His dark brown hair, still damp from his last turn behind the boat, was plastered against his scalp. He'd worked for a lawn maintenance company all summer, and his skin had turned golden brown, the tan emphasizing sharply defined muscles.

As if sensing her gaze upon him, he smiled but didn't open his eyes. Her heart tumbled and her pulse raced.

Erika had fallen in love with Steven the moment she first laid eyes on him. That had been last September, the third week into her sophomore year at Borah High. She'd been heading from her second-period algebra class to her third-period biology class and he'd been walking toward her.

Anna Smith had nudged Erika and said, "Wow! Look at him. Wouldn't I just die to have him ask me out?"

Steven Welby. Senior class president. Track star. All-around athlete. The most popular student in the school. What girl wouldn't just about die?

But Steven hadn't asked Anna Smith out. He'd asked Erika instead. They'd been going together for the past ten months, neither of them dating anyone else since. Considering the short leash Erika's dad kept her on—11:00 P.M. curfew with no exceptions, not even for school dances; no unchaperoned parties; no out-of-town excursions—Erika thought it amazing Steven had stuck around for a month, let alone ten of them.

"You guys thirsty?"

Erika rolled her head to the left.

Dallas Hurst sat up, squinting despite his dark-colored Ray-Bans. "I'm gonna swim over and see what's left in the cooler. Want me to bring you something?"

"Nothing for me," Steven mumbled, sounding as if he'd been asleep.

Erika shook her head. "I'm okay, too."

Dallas was Steven's best friend, had been since they were in first grade, and the two of them were almost always together. Because of it, Erika spent nearly as much time with Dallas as she did with Steven. There were probably some people who didn't know for sure which of them was her boyfriend.

But Erika never could have fallen for Dallas. Not that he wasn't charming or good-looking. In fact, he was *too* charming and *too* good-looking. He always had girls hanging around him, flirting with him, hoping to become his girlfriend. Erika didn't think he'd dated the same girl more than two or three times since she'd known him. Dallas was a player. He didn't waste himself on girls who wanted anything more than a good time.

Dallas stood, stretched, then dived into the water and swam toward shore.

Erika turned her head back to Steven. His eyes were open now, and he was watching her. She felt that wonderful-terrible fluttering sensation in her stomach.

Oh yes. She loved him. Loved him more than life itself. And she was scared because he was going away without promising he would return to her, without asking her to wait for him. He would spend his days with pretty, sexy college girls. Girls who would no doubt be more than willing to give him whatever he wanted.

Had she made a horrible mistake by refusing him when he'd wanted more from her than kisses?

"Come here," he commanded gently.

She rolled onto her right side and into his waiting embrace. He pulled her close, kissing her, slow and sweet, and she wished for another day, another week, another month together. Maybe if she had more time she could make him say he loved her, make him ask her to wait, even make him propose.

Steven drew back slightly, ending the kiss. "Oregon isn't so far. I'll come home for holidays, and we'll see each other then."

"Thanksgiving is three months away."

"It'll go fast."

"No, it won't," she whispered, afraid she might cry. "I'm going to be so lonely."

He kissed the tip of her nose. "Dallas'll be here. The two of you can get together."

"Maybe."

Erika didn't believe it would happen. Dallas would have his hands full with the coeds at Boise State. He wasn't going to have time to spend with Steven's old girlfriend, a mere junior in high school.

Besides, it wasn't Dallas she wanted to be with. It was Steven and only Steven. But he was going away in the morning, leaving her behind with her broken heart.

Erika was certain she'd never be happy again.

CHAPTER ONE

JUNE, TWENTY-THREE YEARS LATER

"OH, STEVEN! Ethan would love it." Erika Welby stared at the automobile—a 1955 red-and-white Chevy Bel Air with pristine whitewalls parked in the car dealership's showroom. "It looks like the one you had in high school. But can we afford it?" She glanced at her husband.

Steven jerked his head in the direction of the garage door. "Ask them. They're the buyers."

Erika whirled about to find Dallas and Paula Hurst standing near the open doorway, both of them grinning like Cheshire cats.

"Don't refuse," Paula pleaded. "We want to do this."

"You know we love the kid." Dallas draped his right arm around Paula's shoulders. "It'll be a great surprise for his birthday."

It would, indeed. Ethan had wanted a car of his own since obtaining his driver's license last year. This one, an exact replica of the car Steven had owned at the same age, would be his dream car. But with college expenses looming on the horizon and a single-income budget, Erika wondered how they would ever pay for it.

"Aren't you the one who's always saying it's more blessed to give than to receive?" Dallas lifted an eyebrow, challenging her. "Are you going to rob us of this blessing?"

A part of Erika wanted to resist. A part of her hated the idea of being indebted to Dallas Hurst for any reason. She had her reasons. Plenty of them. But she'd trained herself years ago to pretend those reasons didn't exist.

Besides, she knew Dallas and Paula could afford to buy the car. They didn't have children, and both of them were successful professionals in their respective fields—Dallas in computers and Paula in real estate development. Dallas, Ethan's godfather, had always doted on the boy. Would it be so wrong to accept his generous offer?

Erika looked at Steven again. His hopeful expression reminded her so much of their son that she had to grin. Steven turned toward his best friend. "Okay."

The two men let out identical whoops and stepped toward each other for a high five. Then they headed off to strike a deal with the salesman.

Paula's laughter drew Erika's gaze. "Do you suppose they'll ever change?" Paula said.

"Never." Erika shook her head.

They were alike in countless ways, those two men. Over the years, they'd played baseball together, tormented their sisters together, learned to golf together, been sent to the principal's office together—just to name a few things. They'd never lived more than five miles apart, with the exception of the time Steven was away at college. When Steven and Erika got married, Dallas had served as best man. And Steven had returned the favor years later.

But they were different, too, and Erika often wished the two men weren't friends at all. There were times when she hated the thought of seeing them together, of listening to their good-natured male banter, of knowing they shared things she couldn't be a part of.

The truth was, Erika was never completely at ease with Dallas. Perhaps because she knew things about him that were better forgotten. And so, as usual, she made the choice to forget, tucking unpleasant thoughts away in some dark corner of her mind.

Paula interrupted her thoughts by asking, "Is this as much like Steve's old car as the guys say it is?"

"Yes." Erika turned toward the automobile. "It's identical. Could be the same one, for all I know." She ran her fingertips along the driver's side door. "Steven kept his car shining clean, like this. He was so proud of it. He worked hard to earn the money to buy it."

A frown puckered her forehead. Would the car mean more to Ethan if he had to work for it the same way his dad had?

"Oh no!" Paula exclaimed. "Look at the time. I've got an appointment in twenty minutes. I'll never make it if the lights aren't with me. Tell Dallas I had to run." She raised her hand in a half wave. "See you Saturday." Then she hurried away, her high heels clicking against the concrete floor.

Feeling suddenly dowdy compared to Paula's ultrachic, ultrafit image, Erika stared after the younger woman.

Paula Hurst—thirty years old, petite, slender, and as pretty as any cover model with her short red hair, cat-green eyes, and pouty lips—lived a high-paced life, a wireless phone in one hand and an electronic organizer in the other. Since the first day Dallas introduced Paula to the Welbys, Erika had never seen her look anything but totally put together—makeup on, hair perfectly coifed, nails manicured.

"I haven't been totally put together since Ethan was born," Erika muttered as she turned toward the Chevy.

Seventeen years. How was it possible Ethan was about to have his seventeenth birthday? Where had the time gone? It seemed only yesterday since she'd cradled that squalling, red-faced newborn in her arms; only a moment since she'd sat in the rocking chair at 2 A.M. and watched him nurse; a second in time since she'd worried about fevers, coughs, and spit-up, healthy baby check-ups, and keeping current with immunizations. When did her baby boy get to be big enough to ride a bike, let alone drive a car?

"I'm going to be blubbering in another minute," she whispered to herself as she closed her eyes. *Thank You, Lord, for the gift of my son.*

She released a deep breath, the brief prayer making her feel better. And not a moment too soon.

Steven jingled the car keys as he reentered the garage. "Sweetheart, we got it. Wanna drive into the foothills and smooch awhile? No bucket seats in this lady."

"Oh, sure. That would set a good example for Ethan, wouldn't it?" But her refusal couldn't dim the pleasure she felt at her husband's suggestion. Truth was, after eighteen years of marriage, Steven still made Erika go weak in the knees. "Besides, you've got to get back to work."

"It's a mighty nice day for a drive," he cajoled. "I could play hooky."

"Is this car for Ethan—" she playfully punched him in the arm—"or are you trying to relive your wild and woolly youth, Mr. Welby?"

He grabbed her and pulled her close. "Both."

Then he kissed her.

AUGUST 1979

As Steven's Chevy rolled to a stop at the curb in front of her house, Erika fought tears. "Here we are," Steven said softly.

She looked toward the house. "Yeah."

"Sorry the movie was such a drag."

"It was okay." She turned to look at him. "I like everything when I'm with you."

He put his right arm around her shoulders. "Me, too." He kissed her temple.

"I wish you weren't going," she whispered, unable to stop herself.

"Hey, you'll be so busy with school, you'll probably forget me in a month."

She swallowed the lump in her throat. "I won't forget you, Steven. I love you."

"I know." This time he kissed her on the lips.

She clung to him, feeling desperate. It hurt that he hadn't said he loved her, too. She knew he cared. They'd been together almost every day this summer, and he'd always treated her special. But he'd still never said he loved her.

Steven broke the kiss just as it was beginning to steam up. "I'd better get you inside," he said hoarsely.

In that moment, she wished she hadn't told him no all those times when he'd wanted more from her. She knew it had been the right thing to do, but still . . . If only she'd given in to his desires, then he would have said he loved her. If only she hadn't been so afraid. If only . . .

Steven opened the car door and got out, then held a hand toward her.

She was crying now, tears sliding silently down her cheeks as they walked toward the front stoop, still holding hands. The porch light, moths fluttering around it, cast a yellow glow on the narrow sidewalk.

"I'll be back for Thanksgiving," Steven said.

It didn't help. This was August, the nights warm and alive with the sounds of crickets. Thanksgiving was in cold and silent November. It seemed a lifetime away.

"I'll write to you, Erika."

"Promise?" she whispered.

Reaching the house, he stopped and turned toward her, placing his hands on her shoulders. "I promise." He smiled. "You're gonna write to me, too. Right?"

She nodded, her throat too thick with emotions to speak.

Don't leave me, Steven. I love you. I need you. Don't go. Please don't go. Say you love me. Say you'll never leave me.

Just as Steven leaned forward to kiss Erika again, the front door jerked open. In unison, the couple turned toward it.

"It's after eleven," Erika's father said gruffly.

"Hi, Mr. James," Steven replied. "Sorry I got Erika home late. The movie ran a bit long."

Her father grunted as he scowled first at Erika, then at Steven.

Steven faced Erika again. "I've gotta go."

"I know," she mouthed, but no sound came out.

"You take care," he said softly. His beautiful blue eyes seemed to offer tenderness, encouragement, hope. "You tell Dallas if you need anything. Okay?"

She nodded, blinking hard to stop the tears.

Steven kissed her lightly on the lips, then strode away.

"That was some show you were giving the neighbors," Erika's father snapped. "I won't stand for it, girl. You understand me?"

"But, Dad, we didn't—"

"Get inside. *Now!*"

She wanted to turn and run after Steven. Instead, shoulders slumping, she followed her father into the house.

CHAPTER *Two*

STEVEN WHISTLED an old Righteous Brothers' tune as he opened the front door to Parker Elementary and entered the building. All was quiet now that school had let out for the summer.

Jessica Shue, the school secretary, lifted her gaze from the papers on her desk. She picked up two message forms and held them out to him. "These are for you."

"Thanks." He took them, glanced at each slip, then continued toward the door with his name stenciled on the milk white glass: *Principal Welby*. He grinned. He couldn't help it. There was something about those two words that made him feel good every time he saw them.

He supposed there were some who considered him less than successful, if not an out-and-out failure. At forty-one, he didn't make a huge salary. He didn't have a large savings account. He didn't own a big house or a fancy boat or an expensive car. What he had was a wife and son whom he loved to distraction, a cozy home with a low mortgage, two cars that they owned free and clear, and a job he enjoyed going to every day.

How many men his age could say that?

He sat in the chair behind his desk, glancing at the messages again. The first was from his pastor regarding the church's annual father-son breakfast. The other was a reminder of his semiannual dental appointment. Neither call needed to be returned.

He swiveled the chair toward the window, looking out at the empty schoolyard. Sprinklers shot arcs of water across the grass. Muddy puddles pooled beneath the monkey bars. Several robins hopped about, searching for worms.

He missed the kids. There was something all wrong about a schoolyard without children playing, shouting, and running. He'd be glad when the session started again in the fall. He always was.

Steven's thoughts drifted to his son. He remembered when Ethan was in grade school. In reality, it wasn't all that long ago—only six years—but it seemed longer. Ethan was becoming a man right before his eyes. He was already an inch taller than Steven and still growing. His voice had lowered before he'd turned fourteen, and this year he'd started shaving regularly.

Cute enough to drive the girls crazy, Ethan was a serious student, carrying a four-point grade average. He was musically gifted and played several different instruments, including the piano and alto sax. He'd starred in this spring's high school production of *A Midsummer Night's Dream*. Like all the men in the Welby clan, Ethan was athletically inclined, although he preferred sports like golf, tennis, and swimming to the rowdier team sports favored by his uncles and cousins.

And now, thanks to the generosity of Dallas and Paula Hurst, Ethan was about to become the owner of a classic '55 Chevy.

Steven grinned. His son would never suspect. It was no secret that Ethan wanted a car of his own, but he'd been saving the money he earned at his part-time job at the hardware store. Everybody expected him to get a scholarship, of course, but Ethan was smart enough to know there would be plenty of other out-of-pocket expenses. He said he'd rather borrow his mom's car or ride his bike than come up short of cash when it came time for college.

That was one of the reasons Dallas had insisted on buying the car. "How many boys Ethan's age are that levelheaded?" Dallas had asked Steven last week. "Maybe you were, but I wasn't. I'm lucky I graduated at all. Too busy partying and making out with the girls." He'd punctuated his sentence with a self-satisfied wink.

Steven turned his chair toward the desk. The truth was, even though Dallas pretended to be a wild child with no cares, Steven could see the longing in his eyes when he looked at Ethan.

Dallas had never said why he and Paula didn't have children after nearly nine years of marriage, and Steven had never asked. What he did know was this—Dallas would make a great dad.

～

Dallas had to call in a few favors in order to get reservations on such short notice at Billet Doux, a popular French eatery in downtown Boise. But he wanted the evening to be perfect, and this was Paula's favorite restaurant.

"Your table is ready, sir," the hostess told him. "Would you like to be seated while you wait for the rest of your party?"

"Please."

The hostess led the way to the patio table he'd requested. She gave him a menu and disappeared back to the front. On the east side of the restaurant, the table had a clear view of the foothills, still green in these early days of June. The evening was pleasant, warm but not hot, and a breeze whispered through the branches of the young trees that encircled the patio.

Dallas removed his suit jacket and draped it over the back of a chair. As he sat down, a waitress approached, order pad in hand, a shimmy in her hips. Probably no more than twenty-five, if that, she was long-legged and lithe with a cascade of ebony hair and big brown eyes. Her gaze slid over him, and when she smiled, Dallas knew he'd measured up despite their age difference. He responded as any red-blooded American male would—with a grin.

"Can I bring you something to drink?" she asked in a voice that was something close to a purr.

"No, thanks." Remembering what had brought him to the restaurant, he added, "I'll wait for my wife."

Her smile slipped. To Dallas, it was an enormously satisfactory reaction.

"I'll check back," she said, "in case you change your mind." The tilt of her head sent a silent message: In case you change your mind *about me.*

Dallas leaned back in his chair, still grinning.

"Do I need to scratch her eyes out?"

He laughed as he looked over his shoulder; Paula stood at the patio entrance, a frown furrowing her brow.

"Caught me looking." He stood and walked over to her. "But don't hurt her. I told her I was waiting for my beautiful wife." He embraced her. "You know no other woman can hold a candle to you."

"See that you don't forget it, buster."

He couldn't tell if she was seriously annoyed with him or not.

He kissed her warmly, then asked, "How was your meeting with Gerard Stone?"

"Henry & Associates will get the loan." She gave her head a little toss. "You know that old goat can't deny me anything."

Dallas laughed again. "Neither can I." He took her by the arm and steered her toward their table.

"I take it you and Steve worked out the deal for Ethan's car after I left the dealership."

He pulled out the chair for her. "Yup. I even talked Steve into letting me drive the Chevy over to his brother's. That's where they're keeping it until the party."

He sat in the chair at Paula's right hand. "I took the long route getting there, and by the time the cab brought me back to the dealer's, I figured there wasn't much point in returning to the office." Twisting toward his jacket on the back of the chair, he reached into a pocket and pulled out a small gold box. "So I did some shopping instead." He slid the box toward Paula.

"Oh, Dallas." Her face lit up. Nobody loved getting presents more than his wife. "What have you done now?"

He had a reason for buying the platinum-and-diamond necklace. A reason beyond the pleasure of hearing her squeal of delight as she lifted the gift from its box.

"Dallas darling, it's exquisite."

He watched as Paula fastened the necklace around her delicate throat.

His wife was thirty, and Dallas would be forty-one in less than two months. They'd agreed to start a family five years ago, but here they were, still childless. Dallas wanted to know why.

Paula hated doctors, needles, hospitals, and medical tests of any kind. For months she'd turned a deaf ear to his not-so-subtle hints that they undergo fertility tests. So, without telling his wife first, Dallas had gone to see his doctor. Today he'd received the results from Dr. Kramer.

Now he needed to find a way to tell Paula that there was nothing wrong with him, that there was no reason he couldn't father children. He had to convince Paula to see her own doctor.

It might take more than one platinum-and-diamond necklace to achieve his objective. Lots more.

CHAPTER THREE

"HEY, MOM!"

Erika turned from the center island in Paula's kitchen, where she was chopping celery on the butcher block.

Ethan stood in the doorway. His wet hair was plastered to his head, and droplets of water glittered on his suntanned skin. "The guys want to know when the burgers'll be ready. We're starved."

"Your dad and Dallas had to run a quick errand. They should be back soon." She lifted a serving dish of olives, carrots, celery, and dip. "I'll bring some snacks out in a few minutes."

He flashed her a grin. "Thanks." Then he dashed back to the swimming pool, where his friends were engaged in a frenzied game of water volleyball.

"It's a good thing the weather held," Paula said, drawing Erika's gaze.

"Ethan appreciates you letting us have the barbecue here. So do Steven and I."

Paula shrugged off the thanks. "You know we're glad to do it. Dallas and I don't use the pool nearly enough. It's good to see somebody enjoying it."

Hearing more animated shouts from outside, Erika laughed softly. "Well, nobody could enjoy it more than a bunch of teenagers."

"So true."

Erika grabbed the sealed tops of three large bags of chips with one hand and balanced the relish tray with the other. "I'll take these out to the table before they start rioting from hunger."

"Maybe I'd better call Dallas and see what's keeping them."

"Yes, maybe you—" Before Erika could finish, she heard voices coming from the front of the house. "That must be them now."

A few moments later, Steven appeared out of the hallway, Dallas right behind him.

Steven grinned from ear to ear. "I parked it over in front of the neighbor's house," he said in a stage whisper, "in case anybody goes out front for some reason." He held up an overnight mail envelope. "I stopped by the house and found this on the front porch. It's addressed to you." He glanced at it. "Name's Lundquist?"

Erika shook her head. "Probably a sales gimmick. Just drop it by my purse there. I'll look at it later. Right now, we've got some starving, waterlogged kids to feed, and you've got burgers to grill."

"Aye, aye, Captain." He saluted her, then tossed the envelope onto the counter as instructed.

It didn't take more than a minute for the pool to empty and the ten teenagers, five girls and five boys, to swarm the picnic table on the patio. There was plenty of good-natured shoving and lots of laughter as the bags of chips were torn open.

Erika stepped back from the feeding frenzy and watched with a sense of pure delight. She loved being with Ethan and his friends. She didn't think there was anything better in the world than being a wife and mother, spending time with her family, sharing love with those closest to her.

"There you go," Steven whispered.

She turned, not surprised to find him nearby.

"You're doing that melodramatic mother thing again." He clutched his hands beneath his chin, lifted his dark blue eyes toward the sky, and in a high-pitched voice said, "Oh, my baby boy is all grown up. Whatever shall I do?"

She playfully slapped his shoulder before leaning into him and sharing a kiss. "I can't help it," she said when their lips parted. "I'm blessed, and I know it. God's been good to us."

"Amen to that." All signs of teasing vanished.

Their gazes held a moment longer; then Steven returned to the grill and his duties as chef while Erika walked toward the kitchen. She reached the doorway as Dallas came out, carrying a cooler full of sodas.

"Your father and grandmother are here," he said.

"Already?" Erika felt the familiar twinge of nerves that came whenever her father was around. Would the food be okay? Would the kids be too rowdy, too noisy? What could go wrong and what could she do to prevent it?

In her father's presence, she became an uncertain, fretful child, wanting desperately to earn his approval. Why, she often wondered, couldn't she change their relationship? Why, when it came to her father, was she stuck in the same rut after all these years?

She entered the kitchen. Trevor James and Louisa Scott, her maternal grandmother, were both seated in the breakfast nook.

"Hi, Dad." She smiled. "Hi, Grams."

Her father acknowledged her greeting with a slight nod of his head.

Her grandmother—still spry at eighty-two—motioned her closer. "My goodness, Erika. Aren't you pretty as a picture. I swear, you look like a teenager yourself in that outfit."

"Oh, Grams. Don't be silly." She kissed the sweet woman on the cheek.

Erika often wondered how she would have survived childhood if not for her grandmother's love. After Erika's mother, Mary James, died of complications from pneumonia when Erika was ten, Louisa Scott—a widow herself—had moved in with them in order to care for Erika. Through all the years since, Louisa had been there whenever Erika needed her. And some of those years had been pretty rough.

"The burgers are on the grill," Erika said to the room

in general, her gaze flickering to her father, then away again. "It shouldn't be long before they're ready."

Paula opened the refrigerator. "I'll take the salads out to the mob."

"Where's Ethan?" Trevor interjected gruffly. "Isn't he going to come say hello to his grandfather?"

"He doesn't know you're here, Dad." Erika despised the quaver in her voice. "I'll tell him."

She went outside, glad to get away, and crossed the patio, her hands clenched into fists at her sides.

OCTOBER 1979

Erika lay on her back on the bed, telephone pressed to her right ear, her left ankle resting on her bent right knee.

"I haven't had a letter from Steven in three weeks," she told Anna.

"Why don't you go out with somebody else? That'd serve him right."

Erika sighed. "I don't want to date anybody else. I love Steven."

"You know what, Erika? You need to get a life. I always thought Steven was cool, too, but the dude's gone off to Oregon. So get over it. There's plenty of guys right here in Boise who'd love to take you out."

"Name one."

"How about Dallas Hurst? He's a stud muffin."

"Dallas? He's not interested in me."

"Well, he's sure hangin' around your place a lot for a guy who's not interested."

Erika knew she couldn't make Anna understand the way things were between her and Dallas. They spent time together partly out of habit, partly because they both missed Steven. That was all.

Anna abruptly switched the subject. "Are you going to the Halloween dance on Friday?"

"No." Erika rolled onto her stomach, bracing herself on her elbows. "I wasn't planning to."

"Come on, Erika. Tommy and I'll pick you up. You won't have to go alone."

"I don't think so, but thanks anyway."

"You need to get over it, Erika James." There was a pause; then Anna said, "My mom's calling me. Gotta go."

"Talk to you later."

Erika hung up the phone, then reached for the single piece of spiral notebook paper that lay on the bed beside her. She idly plucked at the ragged left edge as her eyes scanned the words she already knew by heart. *Dear Erika,* Steven had written.

How's it going? You keeping your grades up? I'm doing okay. I like Eugene, but it sure rains a lot. People even wash their cars when it's raining. They say if you don't, you'll never

wash it. Guess they're right. College is
tougher than I thought it would be. I
spend most of my free time at the library.
My parents drove over last week and went
to the football game. I think they really
came to be sure I wasn't starving or
spending all my money on something I shouldn't.
You know how parents can be. I may not
make it home for Thanksgiving. Looks like
I might have a job at a local record shop. If
I do, I'll be working straight through the
semester. But I'll be sure and call you as soon
as I do get into town. You take care.
                                    Steven

Erika tried hard to find an "I love you" written
between the lines, but she couldn't.

She wanted to die.

"Erika, dearest," her grandmother called, her
voice muffled through the closed bedroom door.
"Supper's ready."

Erika quickly refolded the letter and slipped it
beneath her pillow, then rushed out of her
bedroom and into the kitchen.

Erika's father was already seated at the table.
He glanced at her and said, "Why weren't you
helping Louisa with supper?"

"Sorry, Dad. I . . . I was on the phone talking to
Anna. I forgot the time."

"Blasted contraption," her father muttered.

Grams lifted a platter of fried pork chops from the kitchen counter. Erika hurried to take it from her, then carried it to the table where she placed it in front of her father before taking her seat to his left. Grams joined them, sitting in her chair at the foot of the table.

"I want this moping around to stop," her father said as he dished vegetables onto his plate. "Do you hear me?"

"Yes, Dad."

"Sit up straight."

Erika stiffened her spine and squared her shoulders.

"You listen to me, girl. I let you see that Welby boy against my better judgment. I could see how you were around him. Well, he's gone now, and good riddance. The way you were going, it's a miracle you didn't get yourself in trouble. Your whole generation's going down the drain, and I mean to see to it that you don't go right along with them."

"Trevor, please," Grams said softly.

"Stay out of it, Louisa. You know I'm right."

"Erika's never given you any cause to believe—"

"I said, stay out of it."

Grams pressed her lips together in a firm line.

Erika stared down at her plate, biting her lip. Why did it always have to be this way? "I haven't done anything I shouldn't, Dad. Honest."

"See that you don't." He shoved the vegetable dish in her direction.

The rest of the meal was eaten in silence.

CHAPTER FOUR

STEVEN AND DALLAS WATCHED as Erika walked toward the picnic table. Her face was pale, her movements stiff.

"Your father-in-law's here," Dallas said.

"Yeah." Steven turned back to the grill. "I could tell."

"How do the two of you put up with him? He's the coldest fish I've ever met."

Steven didn't answer, even though he'd thought much the same thing about Trevor James over the years. The same and worse besides. In fact, there was only one good thing he could say about his father-in-law, and that was that he loved his grandson. Of course, everybody warmed to Ethan. He was a kid with a winning manner that even his grandpa couldn't resist.

But Erika was special, too, and why the man couldn't

be decent to her Steven would never understand. He thought of the many times he'd held his wife in his arms while she cried over something her father had said or done.

Even on their wedding day.

As though it were yesterday, he remembered standing in the reception line, his left hand on the small of Erika's back, while well-wishers congratulated them. Steven had felt like the luckiest man alive that day. Judging by Erika's smile, he knew she'd felt the same.

Then Trevor had announced to all within hearing that it was just as well Erika got married because her grades had never amounted to much. "Sheer waste of money to send her to college. Not smart enough to make more of herself. Best thing about this day is now she's somebody else's headache."

Steven remembered her brave expression as Erika had fought to keep smiling through the rest of the reception, not letting down until the newlyweds were finally alone. Then she'd cried.

"Why can't I ever please him?" she'd asked between sobs.

"Forget what he said, Erika. You please me. I know you're smart, as well as pretty and loving and desirable." He'd tilted her chin with his index finger, forcing her to meet his gaze, hoping to tease away her tears. "You gotta be smart. You chose me for your husband, right?"

It had worked, more or less, but he knew the hurt never quite left her.

"Has the old coot retired yet?" Dallas asked, pulling Steven back to the present.

"Not yet."

Dallas took a swallow of soda. "How old is he, anyway?"

"Seventy this year."

"No way that's gonna be me. I'm planning for early retirement. Maybe by fifty-five." His gaze drifted to Paula, who was talking to Ethan's friends. "Of course, that could change soon. Kids're expensive."

"Kids?" Steven's eyes widened in surprise. "Is Paula pregnant?"

His friend was silent for a few moments, then answered, "Not yet, but we're hoping."

Steven wasn't sure what to say next.

"We haven't done anything to prevent it for a long time. Years actually. It didn't matter at first. We were both building our careers. I figured when the time was right, it would happen, but it never did." Dallas cleared his throat. "I went for some tests. You know. To see if anything was wrong."

Steven kept his eyes on the grill.

"The doctor says I'm okay." Dallas cleared his throat a second time. "Now Paula's going to make an appointment with her gynecologist."

At last, Steven glanced toward his friend. "I'll say a prayer for the both of you."

"Sure. No skin off my nose." Dallas shrugged, then said, "Those burgers look ready. I'll get the buns." He tossed his empty soda can into the trash receptacle, then strode toward the kitchen.

Steven grabbed a platter and began scooping hamburgers onto it. Moments later, he carried it to the picnic table. The rest of the adults joined the teenagers on the patio, and for a while, chaos reigned.

⁂

Erika smiled at her husband as he settled beside her on a lounge chair, balancing a paper plate on his knees. "They'll all be done eating pretty soon."

"Like a swarm of locusts." He chuckled. "Do you think they tasted anything before they inhaled it?"

"Maybe a little." She leaned toward him, whispering, "When do we give Ethan the car?"

"Just before the other kids leave. Otherwise, it'll break up the party early. He'll want to take it for a drive as soon as he gets those keys in his hands."

She gazed toward the lawn where the teenagers sat, Ethan in the middle of the group. Her son was a handsome young man, but what mattered to Erika was that he had a good head on his shoulders and a tender heart. He'd given them little trouble in his teen years, unlike the children of some of their friends.

"Are you fixing to get all sappy on me again?" Steven asked softly.

"No." But she was. Her eyes were beginning to mist.

"Here's some news that will shock you. Dallas and Paula are trying to have a baby."

He was right. That *did* shock her. Erika turned to look at Steven, blinking to clear her vision. "Really?"

"Paula didn't say anything to you?"

"Not a word." Erika had a difficult time imagining

Paula awake at two in the morning with spit-up on her nightgown. She wasn't exactly the type to reach for another woman's infant or exclaim over cute baby clothes in a shopwindow.

"I told him I'd pray for them."

"What did he say to that?"

"The usual." Steven shook his head. "I wish just once he'd listen to what happened to me—to *us*—when we came to Christ. He's got to see how different we are now from the way we were before. After ten years, he's got to know the change is real. We're way past the religious-fanatics, passing-fad stage."

Erika placed her hand on his upper arm. "Don't lose hope."

They were silent for a short while before Steven said, "I've always known Dallas would make a great dad."

She supposed Dallas would make a good father, but she didn't want to discuss it with Steven. Some things were better left alone.

Steven continued, "Dallas said he went to the doctor to make certain he wasn't the reason Paula hasn't conceived. I guess he got the all clear. Now it's Paula's turn."

Erika rose abruptly from the lounge chair. "I need a soda. Want anything?" She walked away before he could answer.

೩

Dallas didn't think he'd ever seen his godson dumbstruck. Unlike a lot of boys his age, Ethan had plenty of self-

assurance, a quick wit, and a large vocabulary. He always
had something to say.

But when Ethan saw that red-and-white Chevy and
his dad dropped the keys into his hand, he stood in the
street, staring, mouth agape, while his friends whooped
it up behind him.

Erika gave her son a hug. "Don't you have anything to
say to Dallas and Paula?" she asked, laughter in her voice.

The boy turned. His mouth worked but no words
came out.

Dallas laughed. "You're welcome."

"But I—"

"You keep your grades up and get that scholarship
to Yale. That'll be thanks enough."

Ethan finally moved. He strode over to Dallas and
gave him a tight hug. Then he did the same to Paula,
followed by his dad and his mom.

"Can I take Cammi home in it?" the boy asked of no
one in particular.

"It's your car, honey," Erika answered. "You don't
have to drive my minivan again."

Ethan turned toward the pretty blonde who was
standing close by. "Ready to go?"

"Sure!" Cammi answered.

Dallas was amused by how quickly a group of ten
friends broke into couples, all of them eager to get away
from the watchful eyes of adults. In minutes, they'd gathered their belongings and left in five separate cars.

"You spoil that boy," Trevor James told Erika loud
enough for the next-door neighbors to hear. "There are

plenty of other things you could do with your money than spend it on some blamed car."

The light of enjoyment vanished from Erika's eyes. "It wasn't our money, Dad."

Her father grunted as he turned toward his mother-in-law. "Louisa, get your things. It's time I took you back to the center."

Dallas barely kept from grinding his teeth. He couldn't stand that man. Never could. Trevor James had made Erika's youth miserable. For that matter, he'd done his best to make her adult years miserable, too. It was no wonder Erika was so insecure. "Are you going to stand there all day," Paula asked, intruding upon his thoughts, "or help us clean up?"

Dallas looked at his wife.

"I'll do the dishes," she said with a smile, "and you can clean the grill."

When you and I have kids, they'll never have to wonder if their dad and mom love them. They'll know it.

He put his arm around Paula's shoulders. "Sure, let's get it done so everybody'll go home and we can be alone."

$\mathcal{N}$OVEMBER 1979

"Your old man's really something," Dallas said. "You know that?"

Erika shrugged. She didn't want to talk about her dad.

The waitress arrived just then, setting their two large Cokes on the table before them. "Anything else?" she asked.

"No, thanks." Dallas gave her a grin.

The waitress—a woman old enough to be his mother—lit up like a Christmas tree. She looked at Erika and said, "Honey, you better hang on to this one. He's a tiger."

"Hear that, Erika?" Dallas said after the waitress left. "Hang on to me 'cause I'm a tiger." He tried out his sexy smile on her.

It didn't work.

It wasn't that Erika didn't know how handsome Dallas was with his inky black hair, olive complexion, and coppery brown eyes. He could've been a model with his looks and build if he'd wanted to, only he was too busy wowing the girls.

Erika was glad Dallas had never seriously tried turning his immeasurable charm on her. It would have been a waste of time. She was Steven's girl. Or at least, she thought she was Steven's girl. It was hard to know for certain, seeing as how she hadn't heard from him in almost a month.

Dallas leaned back in the booth. "Man, I gotta tell you. There's times I wish I was back in high school. It was sure a lot easier. My folks are always asking about my grades and warning me about the evils of booze and pot." He took a drink of his soda. "College would be a lot more fun if Steve was here."

"Have you heard from him lately?" Erika asked, trying her best to sound nonchalant.

"Nope. Not a word."

"Me, either."

"I should've gone away to school, too. Must be nice for Steve, not having his parents in the same town. He's probably partying down every night of the week."

That's what Erika was afraid of.

"Hey, don't look so heartbroken, kid. It's not the end of the world." He leaned forward. "Speaking of parties, Nora and I've been invited to a bash next Friday. Why don't you and a friend come along? You can see what the college scene is like."

Erika shook her head.

"Come on. It might cheer you up. Besides, it'd really blow your old man's mind. He's always riding your case. He thinks you're doing all sorts of stuff anyway. Might as well be hanged for something you did instead of something you didn't do."

There was a weird kind of logic in what he said.

"You think Steve's hanging around the dorm every Friday night?" Dallas added.

That hurt. Erika shifted in her seat. Thoughts of Steven in the arms of some gorgeous coed swam in her mind once more. Suddenly all of her loneliness, all the broken pieces of her heart, made her want to strike back.

"Okay," she said. "I'll go."

CHAPTER FIVE

ERIKA LAY IN BED, enjoying that pleasant place between sleep and wakefulness. Butter-colored sunlight slipped past the mini-blinds and inched across the bedroom ceiling, a reminder that it was time she was up. But it was far too pleasant to lie there, enjoying her husband's embrace.

"Are you awake?" Steven whispered, his breath warm on the back of her neck.

"Mmm."

"Want me to make coffee?"

She let her eyes drift closed. "Would you mind terribly?"

"No, I don't mind," he answered. But he didn't rise.

Erika smiled. This was their normal Sunday morning ritual, and she loved it for its familiarity.

"What's the time?" Steven asked.

She glanced at the clock radio. "Almost seven."

He groaned. "We'll never make the adult class if we don't get a move on."

"I know."

Still, neither of them moved.

Steven kissed her nape again. "Great party yesterday."

"Ethan loves the car."

"He sure does. He's probably out in the garage, polishing it now."

Erika rolled toward Steven. "I doubt it," she said as their gazes met. "He didn't get in until midnight."

They kissed, sighed in unison, then rolled toward their respective sides of the bed.

"Go ahead and shower," Steven said. "I'll get the coffee started."

"Thanks, hon." Erika pushed her hair away from her face. "I won't be long."

"Leave me a little hot water for a change. Please."

His words were also part of their routine, and Erika laughed in response. If Steven hadn't managed to break her habit of taking long, hot showers after eighteen years of marriage, it wasn't going to happen.

By the time Erika got out of the shower stall, the mirror was thoroughly fogged and the air muggy. After drying off, she tuned the radio to her favorite contemporary Christian station and sang along with Ray Boltz.

"Coffee's almost ready," Steven announced as he entered the bathroom. He slid open the shower door. "Is there any hot water left?"

"Some," she answered with a laugh before heading for the kitchen.

Moments later, with a supersized mug of steaming coffee in hand, she padded on bare feet to stand near the kitchen window that faced their backyard.

Flowers blazed in a variety of colors, shapes, and sizes. Sparkling with morning dew, the recently mowed grass was a deep emerald green, as was the hedge along the back fence. A few weeks ago, Erika had seen a new nest in the upper branches of one of the globe willows. They would soon have baby birds flitting about the yard.

Oh, how she loved the month of June.

"Morning, Mom."

She turned at the sound of Ethan's voice.

Wearing an oversized T-shirt and a pair of baggy black shorts, her son shuffled into the kitchen. His eyes were half closed. His dark hair stuck out in all directions, the cowlick he'd inherited from his mother especially evident at the moment.

"I didn't expect you to be up yet."

Ethan opened the fridge and lowered his head behind the door. "I promised Cammi I'd pick her up for church." He reappeared, juice carton in hand. "This afternoon, I figured I'd put a wax on the car. Cammi's going to help."

Erika smiled, thinking Steven hadn't been wrong about the polishing by more than a few hours. "Seems like Cammi's over here a lot."

"Yeah," he answered. "I guess so."

She wondered if they were getting too close. They

were at a dangerous age and much too young to rush a serious relationship. Of course, they weren't as young as Erika had been when she had fallen in love with Steven.

Which, she supposed, was precisely the point.

"Dad said he left something out here for me." Ethan crossed to the small built-in desk and riffled through the papers beneath the wall phone. "Have you seen it? You know. Registration and stuff." He held up an oversized envelope. "This it? It's got your name on it."

"No. I completely forgot about that." She held out her hand to take the envelope. "I think what you're looking for is in the drawer."

While her son continued his search, Erika looked at the return-address label. *K. Lundquist.* She didn't know any Lundquists, and she certainly didn't know anyone in Pennsylvania.

She set down her coffee mug, then took the scissors from the organizer caddy and cut open one end of the Tyvek envelope. Inside was a single sheet of plain white stationery.

Dear Mrs. Welby, it began. *My name is Kirsten Lundquist. I was born in Boston on August 1, 1980, and I was adopted when I was three days old. . . .*

The room began to swim. Erika grabbed for the back of a kitchen chair.

. . . born in Boston on August 1, 1980 . . .

Her hand missed the chair. Her knees gave way, and she sank to the floor.

"Mom!"

She lifted her gaze from the white sheet of paper.

Ethan was kneeling beside her. Her mouth tasted like metal. A whirring noise hummed in her ears.

"Mom?"

. . . I was adopted when I was three days old . . .

Ethan grasped her shoulder. "Mom, what's wrong?"

Kirsten.

All these years, in a secret corner of Erika's heart, she'd wondered, and now she had her answer.

Her name is Kirsten.

"Dad, get in here quick!" Ethan shouted. "Something's wrong with Mom!"

Erika pressed the sheet of paper to her chest. "I'm all right," she whispered. But it was too late. Steven came rushing into the room. "I'm all right," she said again, louder this time.

Her husband's gaze met hers, flicked to the clutched stationery, then came back to her eyes again.

Erika felt a shiver of dread.

How could she tell Steven? How, after so much time had passed? She'd stopped fearing this moment a lifetime ago. She'd stopped believing she would have to face it one day. She'd conveniently forgotten that silence could be a lie.

But now—

"Erika?" Steven stepped toward her.

She shook her head.

He looked at Ethan.

"I don't know, Dad. She was reading something, and all of a sudden she collapsed. Sat right down where she is now."

Somehow Erika managed to get to her feet. "I'm fine. I . . . I just need a few minutes alone." Then without any further explanation, she hurried to the master bathroom and locked herself in.

～

Steven didn't know what he'd read in Erika's eyes a few moments before, but he knew he didn't like it. Fear of the unknown twisted his gut as he bent to pick up the envelope. Who was this K. Lundquist? What was in this envelope that caused Erika's peculiar reaction? Or were the two things even related?

"Dad?" Ethan questioned.

Steven shook his head. "I don't know, Son."

"Maybe I should call Cammi. I was supposed to drive her to church but—"

"No. You do as you planned. When your mom's ready to tell us what's up, she will." Was he trying to convince Ethan or himself? "She'll let us know if she needs us."

"If you're sure."

Steven glanced at his son, hoping his expression revealed calm assurance—something he didn't feel in the least. "I'm sure." He strode toward the coffeepot, took a mug from the cupboard, and filled it with the dark brew from the carafe.

The moment he heard Ethan leave the kitchen, he set down the mug, then leaned his hands on the countertop and closed his eyes.

*Lord, I don't know what's going on, but help us . . .
whatever it is.*

DECEMBER 1979

The Boise airport was packed, holiday travelers
coming and going, the mood of most everyone
cheerful and expectant.

Most everyone but Erika James.

She walked beside her grandmother, clutching a
small carry-on bag in one hand, her gaze fastened
on the floor a few strides in front of her. Her
stomach rolled, and she wondered if she was
going to throw up again.

"My cousin Hattie will meet you at the Boston
airport tonight," Grams said. "She'll be holding a
placard with your name on it, but you won't be
able to miss her. She's a very large woman."

Erika swallowed the lump in her throat.

"I wish I could go with you, dearest."

"Me, too, Grams."

"I'll call you every week."

Erika had never been on a plane before. She'd
never traveled far from home. And now she was
headed to the other side of the country.

How did this happen to me? How?

But she knew how.

"Do you think Dad suspects anything?" Erika asked softly.

"No. He's angry with me for insisting on sending you and says a fancy boarding school's a waste of money. But he believes I'm doing it because you're depressed. That's all."

Erika stopped abruptly. "Oh, Grams, I'm scared."

Her grandmother took hold of one of Erika's hands. "I know you are, but it's going to be all right. I'd give my right arm to have this not happen to you. You know that." She squeezed Erika's fingers. "But it did. God will see you through if you'll let Him. He loves you, dearest."

Erika strongly doubted God wanted anything to do with an unwed, pregnant, teenage girl. After all, what she'd done was a sin, according to those televangelists her grandmother liked to watch. But she hoped God *did* care and *would* forgive her—because if her dad ever found out, he'd kill her and send her to heaven himself.

CHAPTER SIX

ERIKA SAT ON THE EDGE of the bathtub, her eyes tightly closed, her breathing shallow, her thoughts far, far away. In another place. In another time.

She was a teenager again, pregnant with a child she wouldn't—*couldn't*—keep. Only her grandmother and their Massachusetts relatives who took Erika in, giving her a place to live for nearly seven months, knew she would soon give birth. Afterward, she would stay in Boston and live at a boarding school to finish her education. Thanks to her grandmother, no one back home would know about Erika's rash mistake, about her betrayal of Steven, the person she loved most in all the world.

She hadn't known that the baby's birth would leave a permanent, if invisible, scar upon her memories, a missing piece taken from her heart. She hadn't known she would often wonder about that tiny girl, born so far from Erika's hometown, left behind to be adopted while Erika went on with her life as if nothing had happened.

And I've lived a lie ever since.

At first, the lie had been because she was young, ashamed, selfish. Later, she'd convinced herself that telling the truth would have hurt too many others.

Especially Steven.

No, she'd thought, it was water under the bridge with nothing to be gained and too much to lose by revealing the secret.

Only now the secret was revealing itself.

O God, how do I explain it now?

She opened her eyes and stared toward the locked bathroom door. She knew her husband was waiting for her to come out, to tell him what was wrong. She knew he was worried.

But how could she tell the man she loved about the secret she'd kept from him all those years? What about Ethan? What about her father and grandmother? What about . . . ?

Help me, Lord.

Drawing a deep breath, she finally looked at the letter again.

Dear Mrs. Welby,
My name is Kirsten Lundqvist. I was born in Boston on August 1, 1980, and I was adopted when I was three days old by Felix and Donna

Lundqvist. After months of research, I've come to believe I'm your daughter.

I decided to search for the identity of my birth parents not because I've been unhappy with my life but because a friend of mine got sick and found out what she had was hereditary. So I came to believe that knowing my birth family's medical history would be wise insurance, just in case something similar happened to me. But the longer I searched, the more curious I became to know more about you and my birth father.

After learning your identity, I wasn't sure whether or not I was ready to contact you. I couldn't be sure you'd be ready to hear from me, either. I put everything away for a long time.

But now the advertising company I work for has merged with another corporation, and the new headquarters is located in Boise. My transfer is effective on the first of July. I knew I couldn't move there and not contact you. I guess it feels like fate stepped in. Maybe we're destined to meet.

I don't know the complete circumstances surrounding my birth, but I know you were only seventeen when I was born. I've got to believe you did what you thought was best for me, given how young you were. I've got many questions because there were only a few nonidentifying details the adoption agency would tell me. I'd like to know the name of my father. I'd like to know if I have any brothers or sisters.

I wonder if you have questions to ask me, too.

I hope you'll agree to meet with me. If so, you can call any of the numbers listed on the enclosed business card. My new mobile phone number is written on the back. I'm leaving Philadelphia on June 21.

It's taken me a long time to write this letter, and I know you might need more time to accept what's in it. Even so, I'll be eager to hear from you anytime.

With warm regards,

Kirsten M. Lundqvist

Erika carefully closed the letter, creasing the fold between thumb and index finger again and again.

"I can't tell Steven," she whispered. "I can't. It would only hurt him. It can't serve any good purpose. And Ethan. What will it do to Ethan?"

What choice do you have?

She pressed her hands against her ears. "I'm not ready. It's too late. I did the right thing."

Like a drowning person, scenes from her life flashed in her mind: The day Steven called to ask her out after he returned from college. The night he proposed. Their cold and snowy wedding day. The joyous morning she realized she was pregnant with Ethan. The night of their son's birth. Their fifth anniversary. Their tenth anniversary. Their fifteenth.

It was all there. All the struggles and triumphs, joys and sorrows. Her life.

And this girl had no part in it. No part.

She crumpled the letter.

"I won't tell him. I won't answer her. Let her think she's mistaken."

She's your daughter.

"No." She shook her head. "She's someone else's daughter. She's the daughter of the woman who raised her. Not mine." She looked upward. "You wouldn't ask me to do this. You couldn't possibly want me to do this. Not when my family could be at risk. I won't hurt them this way. I won't."

She stood, then went to the sink and splashed water on her face, hoping to remove all traces of tears.

It seemed an eternity to Steven before Erika emerged. Her face was pale, her eyes puffy from crying. She moved carefully, as if a wrong step would cause her to shatter.

When Ethan was born, they'd come close to losing Erika. She'd hemorrhaged, and for a time, her life had hung precariously in the balance. Steven had been scared to death, knowing he couldn't make it without her.

He felt that same fear now as he watched his wife move toward him.

"Where's Ethan?" she asked softly. "Is he in his room?"

Steven shook his head. "I told him to go on to church. Cammi was waiting for him and—"

"We should go, too."

He stood. "Don't you think you'd better tell me what's wrong?"

"Nothing's wrong."

"Erika—"

"*Nothing* is wrong, Steven."

The edge in her voice, the look in her eyes, said *Back off*. They'd been married too long for him not to recognize it. Yet this was different. This time she was lying to him. Something *was* wrong. He knew it in his gut.

He took a step toward her. "What was in the letter?"

She met his gaze. "I can't tell you. It . . . it would betray a confidence."

"Who is K. Lundquist?" he pressed.

She lowered her eyes. "Someone I knew many years ago."

"Bad news, I take it. About your friend?"

She nodded.

"How does it concern you?" he asked.

She turned away. "We're going to be late to church."

Steven tried to reassure himself. Erika had always been an open book with him. If she said she was keeping a confidence, then she was. Perhaps someone was dying or in trouble with the law. Whatever it was, this Lundquist in Pennsylvania had asked Erika to keep it private.

Okay, if she said she couldn't tell him, then she couldn't tell him.

He grabbed the Tyvek envelope from the table and tossed it into the trash can.

CHAPTER SEVEN

AS IF SHE WERE SIXTEEN AGAIN, Erika laid her cheek upon her grandmother's knee and wept while Louisa Scott stroked her hair and murmured soft words of encouragement. It seemed forever before Erika's tears ran dry and her sobs turned to tiny hiccups.

"You'll come through this," Grams said with a note of confidence. "You'll see. All will be well."

Erika lifted her head and met her grandmother's gaze. "I lied to Steven, Grams. All these years, I've lied to him by my silence, and now I've looked him in the eye and lied to him all over again."

"Yes, you did. But your husband's a good man. He'll find it in his heart to forgive you."

"I'm not so sure. If he finds out—"

Grams cupped Erika's chin with a gnarled hand. "He mustn't just *find* out, dearest. You must *tell* him."

Erika nodded.

"You must tell Ethan, too."

Erika felt a fresh wave of tears welling inside her. She got to her feet and paced the length of the room, ending at a cluttered bookcase.

"You don't have a choice," her grandmother said. "The cat's out of the bag or about to be."

"Ethan will be so ashamed of me."

"Balderdash! That boy couldn't be ashamed of you, no matter what you did."

"Oh yes, he could." Erika turned. "And I couldn't blame him. I've lived a lie before him, Grams. I've let him think I was a virgin when his father and I married. I've stressed the importance of him staying pure until he gets married. I've let him—" The words were cut short by a sob.

"Erika—" Grams pointed at her with an arthritic finger, then at a nearby chair—"come over here and sit down."

She obeyed.

Her grandmother went on in a stern voice. "Now, you listen to me. You've got a lot of things to think about. I know it seems as if the world's spinning in the wrong direction, but it isn't. God's in control of His universe." She narrowed her eyes. "Do you believe that?"

"Yes," Erika whispered, fearing she didn't really believe.

Grams sighed as she leaned back in her chair. "We

can't undo the past, you nor I, but we can trust God with the future."

Erika swallowed hard.

"I'm not saying either one of us always made the right decisions," her grandmother continued. "But we did the best we knew how at the time. Your father can be a hard man, Erika. We both know it. I don't see that we had another choice but to send you away back then, considering everything." She shook her head slowly, her voice dropping. "Maybe your father would've been different if your mother'd lived. I don't know. He just is who he is."

Erika closed her eyes, trying to ignore the cruel twist in her belly.

"You'll have to tell all of them, dearest. Even your father."

"Not if I don't choose to meet the girl."

"Oh, Erika." Grams clucked her tongue. "You won't be able to refuse her request."

"I'm not so sure."

"Aren't you? I am. She'll be living in Boise. Knowing that, yet not knowing her, would drive you crazy." Her grandmother sighed again. "How often I've wondered about her through the years. How often I've prayed that she was loved and cared for and happy."

Erika looked at her grandmother. "You have? I never knew that, Grams."

"You've wondered about her and prayed for her, too."

She didn't want to admit that it was true, but the words escaped her. "Yes, I have."

It wasn't possible, she supposed, for a woman to

carry a life inside her for nine months and not remember it through all the years that followed. She'd been too young and scared, alone and ashamed, to raise a child. Still, there had been moments when she'd felt her baby move inside her swollen belly that she'd wished she could keep her. And there had been times in the years since when she'd wondered what would have happened if she'd made a different choice.

My dad would've killed me. That's what would've happened.

And Steven? What would Steven have done if he'd known?

"You should call Kirsten soon."

Erika stood. "I'll have to think about it." She leaned down and kissed her grandmother's wrinkled cheek, then straightened. "Thanks for listening."

Louisa Scott's gaze was tender, her smile patient. "I'm here whenever you need me."

"You always have been here for me, Grams."

*A*UGUST 1983

A full moon bathed the foothills in a blanket of white light as Steven drove his Chevy along Highway 21. Erika didn't have to ask to know where he was taking her.

She cast a surreptitious glance to her left.

She wouldn't have thought it possible, but

Steven had grown even more handsome in the years they'd been apart. Four years. Four long and difficult years.

He'd written to her once while she'd been living in Boston. Her grandmother had forwarded his letter. She hadn't answered. She couldn't have answered.

Then there was only silence. She hadn't expected to ever hear from Steven again. Even after Erika returned to Boise two years earlier, she hadn't run into him or any of his family or friends. It was as if some invisible wall had gone up, protecting her from difficult memories.

Or so she'd tried to tell herself.

Then suddenly, three weeks ago, he'd called her. Right out of the blue. Nothing could have surprised her more than the sound of his voice on the other end of the telephone line.

"How've you been?" he'd asked.

"Fine, Steven. How about you?"

"Great. I guess you know I graduated in May. It looks like I'll have a teaching job this fall."

"Where?"

"Here in town." He'd cleared his throat. "Hey, listen. I was wondering. Would you like to go out with me on Friday? If you're not seeing somebody, that is."

"No, I'm not seeing anybody."

"So, will you? Go out with me, I mean."

She hesitated, wondering what she should do. But, of course, she really had no other choice. Her heart made certain of that. "Yes, I'll go out with you."

Strange, how quickly she'd realized that she hadn't stopped loving him. She loved him more than ever before. He filled her waking thoughts and her dreams. She'd never forgotten the taste of his kiss, the smell of his skin, the sound of his laughter, the twinkle in his eyes.

Steven pulled off the highway and drove to their favorite spot by the reservoir; then he cut the engine. Silence enveloped the car. Moonlight danced across the water's surface, a magical glitter.

"Erika." He twisted on the seat toward her but made no move to draw her into his embrace. "I . . . there's something important I need to say to you."

She felt her pulse quicken, not sure if it was fear or expectation.

"I love you."

Tears welled in her eyes.

"These last three weeks . . . well, they've made me realize how much you always meant to me. I guess I didn't have the brains to realize it back in high school, but I realize it now."

She could scarcely breathe.

"Erika, will you marry me?"

"Oh, Steven," she whispered.

This was it. This was the moment. She needed to tell him. She needed to tell him what had happened after he left for Eugene. She needed to tell him about the awful mistake she'd made and about the baby girl who'd been born to a frightened teenager back East. She needed to tell him everything and then ask his forgiveness.

"I love you, Erika. I'll take care of you and cherish you. I promise you won't be sorry if you marry me."

She couldn't risk losing him. She knew that then. Nothing was worth the risk of losing him. If he didn't know what had happened to her by now, he didn't ever need to know.

"Yes, Steven," she said, her heart in her throat. "I'll marry you. I love you, too."

CHAPTER EIGHT

EVERY MONDAY MORNING during the summer
months, Steven Welby volunteered to work with kids at
the homeless shelter. Most of them didn't have fathers
or, if they did, didn't know where their fathers were.
Poverty was stamped on their faces. Hardship stared
back at the volunteers from eyes that had seen far too
much for their years.

It just about broke Steven's heart.

Today, he and Chad Snyder—one of the elders at
Harvest Fellowship—had brought six boys and four girls,
ages six through eleven, to the park for a game of softball.

"Frank," Steven said to one of the boys, "help Lori
with her shoelaces, will you?"

The ten-year-old nodded, then knelt to help the
little girl.

One thing Steven had noticed was how seldom he met any bullies living at the shelter. Oh, sure. These kids were far from perfect, and there was plenty of anger in more than a few of them. But they rarely seemed to take it out on each other, and the older ones almost always were protective of the younger, whether they knew them well or not.

He turned toward the opened back door of the church van and grabbed a battered cardboard box filled with baseball gloves he'd bought at several secondhand stores a couple of years back. Most were too big for these kids, but it didn't matter much. He'd learned that having gloves, even ill-fitting ones, made them feel more like a real team.

"All right," Chad called. "Let's get these bases in place. Michael, Frank, pace it off from here." He dropped the home-plate bag.

Steven set down the box, then squatted beside it and began to sort through the gloves.

"Some sermon yesterday, wasn't it?" Chad commented.

To be honest, Steven didn't think he'd heard a word at church. He'd been too preoccupied with Erika and that mystery letter. But he replied, "Sure was."

"You and Ethan planning to go?"

Uh-oh. It seemed his lie had found him out rather quickly. "Not sure yet," he bluffed. "What about you?"

"Yeah. Todd and I've never done a missions trip together." Todd, a year younger than Ethan, was Chad's eldest son. "Seems like a good idea. He won't be at home much longer. Not likely to have another chance as good as this one."

Steven wished he knew what his friend was talking about.

"And Vancouver's not all that far away," Chad continued, oblivious to Steven's confusion. "Olivia wouldn't worry as much with us just across the border in Canada. You know how protective mothers can be."

Steven made a noncommittal grunt.

"Hey, Mr. Snyder," Frank hollered from second base. "How's this?"

"Looks good," Chad called back. "Okay, everybody. Gather round. Let's get this show on the road."

Steven felt a twinge of guilt and a tug of relief at the same time. He didn't much care for getting caught in a fib, but neither was he ready to tell his friend *why* he was totally clueless about a missions trip and Vancouver and why Chad's wife, Olivia, wouldn't be worried.

He stood and tried to listen as Chad gave instructions to the children, organizing two teams of five. But his thoughts quickly drifted to Erika and that letter and wondering again what she was keeping from him.

⁀

Kirsten Lundquist froze in midstride at the first strident ring of the telephone. Her letter had been scheduled for a Saturday delivery. Was it silly to hope she might hear something as soon as today?

With heart in throat, she lifted the receiver. "Hello?"

"Hey, Kir."

Disappointment sluiced through her, and she let out the breath she'd been holding. "Oh, it's you, Van."

"Well, nice to hear your voice, too."

"I'm sorry." She sank onto a barstool, about the only empty chair in her apartment. Everything else was buried under boxes and items yet to be packed. "I'm glad you called. It's just, I was hoping it was—" She stopped, afraid she would make matters worse.

"Your birth mother," he finished for her, a hint of aggravation in his voice. "Don't you think you're expecting a lot? To hear from her this soon."

"I don't know what to expect. This is all new to me, too."

There was silence on the other end of the line for several heartbeats; then her boyfriend said, "Want some help with the packing? I've got the day off."

"To tell the truth, I'm down to the stuff I'm better off to do alone. Nicknacks and business papers and so forth." Quickly she added, "But I'd love an excuse to get out for lunch. Would you join me at Trixie's Diner? Say, one o'clock?"

"Sure. See you there."

The line went dead, and Kirsten slowly returned the receiver to its cradle.

That Van thought she was nuts to leave Philadelphia was no surprise. It wasn't as if she had some major position with Maguire & Son. She'd only been working full-time for the company since she finished her business school courses. With a little effort, she could have found a similar position here in Philly for the same or maybe even better money. She knew it and so did Van.

"Idaho!" he'd exclaimed when she told him. "What would you want to move *there* for? You're a city girl, not a cowgirl."

He could be right, but she was going all the same. Fate had brought about this merger between Maguire & Son and Turtle Associates just so she, Kirsten Lundquist, would have employment in Boise, Idaho. What else could it be but the hand of providence, all the stars falling into place, good karma, whatever?

Her gaze fell on the large notebook on the kitchen counter. She reached out and touched the cover but didn't look inside. She didn't need to. She knew the contents by heart.

She'd begun keeping this notebook the day she decided to search for her birth parents. That was nearly two years ago. She was younger than most adoptees who took up the search, and she'd made plenty of mistakes because of her inexperience. But eventually she'd found something: A name.

Erika Welby.

And more than anything, Kirsten hoped her birth mother would help Kirsten find what she'd never had and what she wanted most of all . . .

A father. *Her* father.

$\sim$

The house was as quiet as a tomb when Erika returned from her grandmother's.

What is it I'm supposed to do, Lord?

Erika wandered from room to room, too restless to
settle anywhere, too distracted to accomplish anything.

Perhaps the Lord had deserted her, for she received
no answer to her prayer, no quiet voice speaking in her
heart, no assurance that all would be well.

Finding herself in her bedroom again, she sank onto
the edge of the unmade bed and opened the top drawer
of her nightstand. The corner of the letter that had
started it all was poking out from beneath a book. After
crumpling it yesterday morning, she had smoothed it as
best she could, folded it in thirds, and stuck it beneath
her devotional journal, a book that had remained
untouched last night and this morning.

She closed the drawer.

*O God, I'm sorry, but I don't know if I want to meet her. She's a
stranger to me. What can I give her? I don't have anything to offer.
Wasn't it better the way it was, both of us with our own families?
Why'd she have to write to me now? Why'd You let this happen to me?*

She rose and left the bedroom, eventually wander-
ing into the backyard. Motley, the family dog—an ugly
mutt of questionable breed—ran up to Erika, racing
circles around his mistress, ears flopping, happy to have
company.

"Sit, Motley."

The dog, eyes hidden behind bushy bangs, obeyed.
Erika stroked his head. "What would you do, boy?"
He panted, tongue lolling out one side of his mouth.
"Some help you are."

Unexpectedly, tears flooded her eyes. She sank

onto the ground and began to beat the grass with her fists, feeling fury and frustration by turns.

"It isn't fair. It isn't fair. It isn't, it isn't, it isn't."

Motley managed to lick her salty cheek a couple of times before Erika pushed him away.

Didn't You forgive me, Jesus? Didn't You wash away my sins? Where's Your help now, when I need it most? How can You make something good out of this mess?

She was angry, angry at God, and it frightened her. She'd thought the Lord was supposed to give believers the measure of faith they needed when they needed it. Well, she was coming up dry.

She recalled the words she'd read in James a few days before: *Whenever trouble comes your way, let it be an opportunity for joy.*

That was a nice quotation with wonderful spiritual overtones, but how was a person supposed to be joyful at a time like this? James obviously hadn't foreseen *her* circumstances when he wrote it.

Erika rubbed the bridge of her nose as she squeezed her eyes shut. "I want this to go away. That's all I want. Just make it go away."

CHAPTER NINE

SOMEONE WAS KNOCKING, *knocking, knocking on the door. The corridor leading to the entrance of this house—hers but not hers—was long and filled with shadows. She hurried toward the door at the end of the hallway, but she couldn't seem to reach it. The door moved farther away with every step she took even as the pounding grew louder and louder and louder.*

She ran and ran and ran. She had to stop the knocking before it woke Steven and Ethan. She had to stop the noise before it drove her mad.

If she didn't . . .

If she didn't . . .

If she didn't . . .

Erika came awake with a start, her heart pounding. She turned her head on the pillow. Steven slept, undisturbed, beside her.

O God, make it stop.

She rolled onto her opposite side and looked at the clock: 5 A.M.

Why is this happening? Why?

She closed her eyes and willed her pulse to slow, willed the memories to go away. She didn't succeed at either.

Like an unwelcome guest, a similar dream replayed in her memory. A dream that had plagued her sleeping hours in the week before her wedding. A nightmare warning her that one day her secret would be found out. But she hadn't paid attention to the warning. She'd gone to Steven on their wedding night with her dark secret tucked deep in her heart, fearing discovery but convinced silence was the better way.

Erika looked at Steven once again, caressing her husband's face with her gaze, feeling the guilt afresh.

I should have told you, Steven, but I was so afraid of losing you again. What if I'd told you I'd been pregnant and given the baby up? What if you'd left me? I loved you too much to take that chance.

Tears blurred her vision, and she rolled away, slipping out of bed. She grabbed her cotton robe and put it on as she walked from the bedroom. Seeing Ethan's door ajar, she stopped and looked in.

Her son lay on his back, one arm slung over his eyes. The blanket and top sheet were on the floor at the foot of the bed. She smiled. He'd always done that. Even as a baby he'd kicked off his covers.

She wondered if Kirsten did the same thing.

I can't allow myself to wonder. I can't meet her. What about Ethan? What about Steven? It would hurt them too much. Don't I have to think about them more than myself or even Kirsten? She said in her letter she was not unhappy. She implied she'd had a good home. Better to let sleeping dogs lie.

❧

Later that morning, Steven sat at his desk, staring at a sheet of paper filled with columns of numbers. He couldn't seem to make sense of them. Not while his thoughts kept drifting to Erika.

Before leaving for work, he'd tried again to get her to open up, but all he'd done was make her mad.

"I'm *fine*, Steven," she'd snapped.

It wasn't like her to be moody. It wasn't like her to keep things from him either. The two of them shared everything—their deepest secrets, their hopes and dreams. They were truly soul mates.

He frowned as he let the paper drop to his desk.

Erika had claimed a headache last night and gone to bed early. It was rare that they didn't end the day with a brief sharing of Scripture and a prayer. There was definitely a problem. Why, then, wouldn't she tell him about it? The phone rang, and Steven picked it up. "This is Mr. Welby."

"And this is Mr. Hurst."

"Hey, Dallas."

"Haven't talked to you since the party. Thought I'd check in and see how Ethan's doing with that new car of his."

Steven grinned, glad to think about something besides his wife's worrisome behavior. "He's treating it like the royal steed."

Dallas laughed, then said, "That's what I figured."

"Brings back a few memories, seeing that Chevy parked in the driveway."

"I bet." Another chuckle. "Hey, you free for a round of golf later this afternoon? We could be done by six or six-thirty so you wouldn't be too late for dinner."

He thought of Erika. "No, I'd better not."

Dallas must have heard something in his voice. "What's up?"

"Nothing much," he fudged.

"You sure?"

"Sure, I'm—" He stopped when he realized he was doing exactly the same thing to Dallas that Erika was doing to him. "No, that's not true. Something *is* wrong."

"You're not sick, are you?"

"No," he answered. "It's Erika."

"Is *she* sick?"

"We're both physically fine." He switched the receiver to his other ear, then swiveled the chair toward the window behind his desk. "Some old friend wrote to her. Somebody I don't know, never heard of. Anyway, whatever was in that letter upset Erika, but she won't talk about it."

"Whew," Dallas breathed. "You had me going for a second there, bud. Sounds to me like a woman thing. You know. PMS or something."

But Steven knew better. He'd never seen his wife act this way before.

"You're worried about nothing," Dallas added. "I'll bet you lunch on it."

"Maybe you're right."

"Okay. So we miss that round of golf this afternoon. You go home and get things cleared up with your wife. Then we'll meet for lunch tomorrow and you can tell me how you've been worried about nothing, and I'll pick up the tab. Deal?"

"Deal." He felt a little better, his mood lifted by Dallas's confidence. So he issued his standard invitation. "Then maybe you can join me on Thursday morning for Bible study."

"Fat chance, friend, but you get points for tenacity."

❦

Barb Dobson sat at Erika's kitchen table, a large spiral-bound notebook open before her. The two women—who both served on the women's ministry board at Harvest Fellowship—had been discussing plans for their church's women's retreat for the past hour.

"Sara Connors wants to know if her daughter's old enough to attend this year. Brenda just turned thirteen." Barb lifted her coffee cup and took a sip, then said, "What do you think?"

"I'm not sure," Erika replied. "The focus of the retreat is on God's plan for marriage, and it just might—" Her voice broke and tears sprang to her eyes. She rose from her chair and turned away.

Too late.

Barb was quickly beside her. "What's wrong? What is it?"

All Erika could do was step into her friend's embrace, cling to her, and weep.

Barb began to pray. "Lord, I don't know what's wrong, but my sister's hurting."

O God, help me know what to do, Erika begged silently.

Barb prayed on, gently rubbing Erika's back until, at last, the storm had passed. Then she led Erika to her chair at the table. "I'll get the Kleenex," Barb said softly. When she returned with the box of tissues, she sat next to Erika rather than across from her. "Care to talk about it?"

Erika shook her head as she dabbed her eyes.

"Anything specific I can be in prayer about?"

She swallowed hard, then managed to whisper, "That I'll do God's will and not my own." She looked at her Bible, resting on the table before her. "That I won't be afraid."

Steven awakened at four the following morning and was instantly aware that he was alone in bed. He got up and went looking for Erika, determined that they weren't going to let the silence continue between them. He found her in the living room, their wedding album open on her lap, her cheeks streaked with tears.

It made for a disturbing image.

"Erika, we've got to talk about this," he said from the living-room doorway.

"Yes." She didn't look up. "We do."

He wanted to sit on the sofa beside her, but ever since Sunday, there'd been an invisible barrier around her that forced him to keep his distance. He sat on the chair instead.

Erika moved the album off her lap, then folded her hands tightly, as if in prayer.

A knot formed in the pit of his stomach.

"Steven . . ." She stopped, drew a deep breath, let it out. "Steven, I need you to promise that you'll listen without interrupting. What I have to say isn't going to be easy."

"Whatever it is—"

"Just promise not to interrupt."

The knot in his belly hardened. "All right. I'll do my best."

She looked at her hands. "It begins a long time ago." Her voice lowered. "A lifetime ago."

Say it, Erika. Whatever it is, just tell me.

"Do you remember when you went away to college?"

He narrowed his eyes, trying to figure out where she was headed.

"I was lonely after you left," she went on. "I was so in love, I thought I'd die with you gone."

"You were sixteen."

She looked at him, scolded him with her eyes for interrupting, shook her head.

"Sorry."

"I *was* in love, Steven. As only a sixteen-year-old girl can be, I suppose. But you went away without asking me to wait for you. I was certain I'd lose you to

71

some sophisticated college girl, one who wouldn't . . .
refuse you.

"Dallas missed you, too," she continued, her gaze
dropping to her hands again. "He'd hung around with
you for so many years, he didn't know what to do with
himself once you were gone. He and I spent a lot of time
together, just like the three of us did before you left.
Mostly we talked about you."

Steven felt a twinge of impatience. What did any of
this have to do with that letter?

"Do you remember Nora Calloway?"

"Sure." He ran his hand through his hair. "She was
Dallas's girlfriend the summer after graduation."

"They broke up that November. It happened at a
party. Dallas caught Nora with another guy, and he
exploded. He wasn't used to being dumped by a girl.
Everybody thought there'd be a fistfight."

"His temper's always had a short fuse."

Erika took a deep breath and let it out. "I was at that
party, too. Dallas decided to leave, and he asked me to
go with him, so I did. I was worried about him." She
shook her head. "Neither of us were fit to drive. We'd
both been drinking."

This bit of news *did* surprise Steven. He couldn't
imagine Erika defying her father by going to a party
where alcohol was served, let alone drinking anything.
Unlike many of her high school friends, Erika had always
toed the line.

She sighed, then looked up. As if reading Steven's
mind, she said, "There were a lot of things I did that fall

that would've surprised you. Things I shouldn't have
done. Going to that party was one of them." She paused
for a few heartbeats before adding, "Leaving the party
with Dallas was another."

November 1979

Erika leaned against the jamb of the back door as
Dallas staggered into the family room, banging his
knee on the coffee table on the way. He cursed a
blue streak.

"Where are your parents?" Erika whispered,
glancing toward the hallway as she made her way
inside.

"They took Julie to some school thing in
Pocatello. Won't be back 'til Sunday." He half sat,
half fell onto the oversized sofa, then motioned to
Erika. "Come on and sit down. I won't bite."

"Want me to turn on the light?" she asked, still
speaking softly.

"No. Leave it off."

She stepped inside, closing the door behind
her. The floor undulated beneath her feet, and she
moved cautiously. Why'd she take that last drink?
For that matter, why'd she take the first one? She
wondered if she would be sick as she sat on the
sofa beside Dallas.

Don't let me be sick. Don't let me be sick.

She leaned back, closing her eyes—that only made the spinning worse. She groaned.

"She dumped me," Dallas muttered. "Do you believe that? She dumped me for that jerk Nelson."

Another groan served as her response.

"I liked her a lot, Erika. I thought I might be falling in love with her." He leaned sideways until their shoulders met. "You know how that is."

"Yeah." She leaned into him, their heads now touching. "I know how it is."

She felt so alone. All she'd wanted was for Steven to write to her once in a while. Was that too much to ask? She felt so alone, so misunderstood, so miserable. No matter what she did, it was wrong. Her father was always scowling at her. Steven had left her. There must be something the matter with her that no one but her grandmother could love her.

"I'm glad you were there tonight," Dallas said. "You're all right. You know that?" He shifted, then draped an arm around her shoulders. "You're okay."

She was tired of being afraid. So tired of feeling like nothing.

He kissed her.

Somewhere in the alcohol-muddled recesses of her brain, she knew he shouldn't be kissing her, and she shouldn't be kissing him back. But at least she wasn't alone. For this moment, she wasn't alone and unwanted and unlovable.

ॐ

When it was over, when sanity—however fragile—returned, Erika wept. Not from the pain. From the shame.

She thought of Steven, of the countless times she'd stopped passion from taking them too far. She loved him, and now she'd let his best friend—

Her stomach lurched. With a hand over her mouth, she dashed for the bathroom. She reached the toilet just in time. Sweat beaded on her forehead as she clung to the porcelain commode and retched. When at last there was nothing left to throw up, she collapsed on the cool bathroom floor and wept again.

Dallas tapped on the door. "Hey, kid. Are you okay?"

"Go away, Dallas."

"I've always liked you, Erika. I don't think any less of you 'cause of this, you know."

Maybe not. But she thought less of herself.

Chapter Ten

SILENCE CHILLED THE ROOM. Steven's stomach felt as if it had been through a blender. He wanted to demand she continue. Yet he wanted to tell her to shut up, to not say another word.

Erika rose from the sofa and walked to the window. "I could blame it on lots of things, Steven. The drinking. The loneliness. Our ages." After a few moments of silence, she turned to face him again. Tears streaked her cheeks. "Afterward, I tried to pretend we'd fallen in love, but it wasn't true. The most we'd been was friends, and even that was because of you. Because we both loved you. Within a couple of weeks, we stopped seeing each other altogether."

Steven stood. It couldn't be true. It couldn't. He would have known. They couldn't have kept something like this a secret for all these years.

"But by then," she continued in a hoarse whisper, "it was too late."

Don't say it, Erika. Don't say it. O God, don't let her say it.

"By then I was already pregnant."

೪

Erika held her breath. She could see the disbelief in her husband's eyes turn to confusion, then to denial, then to heartache.

"Pregnant?" Steven shook his head slowly, as if that alone could change what she'd told him.

"Yes."

"Did you have an abortion?" He asked the question in a voice so soft she almost couldn't hear.

"No." She hugged herself more tightly. "I . . . I couldn't do that. Grams helped me go away to have the baby."

"The boarding school? That's why you went back East?"

"Yes."

Steven rubbed the palms of his hands over his face. "I can't believe Dallas refused to marry you. He was kind of wild in high school, but I never thought—"

Her vision blurred. "Dallas never knew I was pregnant. I couldn't tell him. I couldn't make myself call him. We both felt so guilty about what happened between us that we couldn't stand the sight of each other by the time I knew I was pregnant." The words tumbled out, faster and faster. She wanted to get them said. Now that she'd

begun, she needed to confess it all. "I didn't want to
marry Dallas, and I couldn't let my dad know I was
having a baby, let alone bring her home to raise on my
own." She stretched a hand toward him, begging him to
understand and forgive. "I was sixteen and scared and . . .
and I was still in love with you."

"Strange way to show love."

She bit the inside of her mouth. What, after all,
could she say in her defense?

"It's almost funny, you know?" There was no humor
in Steven's voice nor in the slight upward curve at one
corner of his mouth. "Here Dallas was worried there was
something wrong with him, and it turns out he got you
pregnant after only one night."

Erika felt the blood drain from her head. "Steven
. . ." The truth. *O Jesus, how can I say it?* But she had to
tell the truth. The whole truth. "Steven, it—" she leaned
against the windowsill for support—"wasn't only one
night."

"But you said—"

"I tried to make myself believe it wasn't something
sordid, like a one-night stand. I wanted to pretend we
felt more for each other than we did. I had to pretend for
as long as I could. And that meant, when we were
together . . ." She let her words drift into a guilty silence.

After several agonizing minutes, Steven said, "Our
wedding night was all an act for you."

She felt sick.

"You pretended you were shy and unsure. I thought
it was because you were innocent, and all the while—"

his eyes narrowed in disgust—"you were playing me like a cheap guitar."

"No. I never . . . I didn't mean . . . Please, Steven, I need you to understand. I never meant to—"

He turned and strode out of the room.

"Where are you going?" she called, panic in her voice.

"Out."

She wanted to run after him. She wanted to grab him by the arm and force him to talk to her, force him to understand, force him to forgive her. But she didn't move. Perhaps she *couldn't* move. A strange lethargy stole over her, a feeling of emptiness, hopelessness.

"Why, God?" she whispered. "Why now?"

She moved to the sofa and sat down, hiding her face in her hands.

He doesn't know Kirsten's coming to Boise. I didn't get a chance to tell him.

Kirsten.

Her daughter.

Hers and Dallas's.

A groan tore from her throat. She hugged her arms over her abdomen and leaned forward from the waist.

Memories flew at her from every direction.

She remembered how she'd hated Dallas for getting her pregnant, hated him for being Steven's best friend. She remembered how frightened she'd been in Boston, so far from home, how alone and unloved she'd felt. She remembered the pain that had torn through her seventeen-year-old body on the night she went into labor, and she remembered that wrenching moment when the nurse had asked if she wanted to see her daughter before they took her away.

And yes, she remembered her wedding night, remembered wondering if Steven would guess the truth, would know that her body had brought forth another man's child.

O God, what am I to do?

There was a verse in the Bible that said something like, *You may be sure that your sin will find you out,* and another that said *Everything now hidden or secret will eventually be brought to light.*

Both verses seemed to have been written with Erika in mind, and surely both of them had come true today.

Steven got on the freeway and drove, not caring what direction he headed. He rolled the windows down, letting in the fresh air as he barreled down I-84 at seventy-five miles per hour. He needed the cool morning wind to slap against his face. He wished it would slap him harder.

His whole life had been a lie. Everything he believed about himself and his family was a figment of his imagination. What an idiot! As though it were yesterday, he remembered his bride's shy glances on their wedding night, her tentative gestures, her tears. He'd thought her pure and innocent, but she'd duped him. Duped him completely.

And Dallas, the best man at his wedding . . .

Steven set his jaw and gripped the steering wheel as if trying to break it in two.

Dallas was Ethan's godfather, the man who'd promised to look after the boy should anything happen to Steven. Dallas had been privy to all of Steven's hopes and dreams, successes and disappointments.

The lying, stinking cheat.

It had all been an act. A pretense. Dallas had stolen something precious from Steven, and Steven had been too trusting to realize it.

For once in his life, he wished he were a violent man. He wished he could take out his rage on something—or on someone. He wanted to share this pain.

Why had this happened? Hadn't he been honest and upright in the way he lived his life? Hadn't he been a good husband to Erika? Hadn't he treated her with gentleness and love and respect? Hadn't he been faithful to her, even before he knew the Lord? It wasn't as if he'd never had the opportunity to be unfaithful. There were plenty of single moms who passed through his office, and more than one who'd sent out vibes that said, *I'm available.*

But no, that would have been against his marriage vows. It would have been against his values to even think of such a thing. Yet his wife had not only been unfaithful to the man she professed to love, but she had *lied* to him.

She wasn't your wife back then.

As good as, he argued. *She claimed she loved me.*

She was sixteen.

She lied.

She did something stupid.

She betrayed me.

She loves you.

She lied, she lied, she lied.

The car sped past the freeway exits to the towns of Nampa and Caldwell.

She had a baby. Before Ethan, she had another baby. One that isn't mine.

His heart was breaking in two.

He remembered again the day Ethan was born, remembered that terrifying moment when they'd thought they would lose Erika on the delivery table as her life's blood drained away. He remembered the doctor telling him that there was no possibility of more children. Steven would never have another son or daughter. The large family both he and Erika dreamed of had disappeared in that delivery room. Ethan would never have any brothers or sisters.

Only Ethan *did* have a brother or sister.

Which is it?

Steven couldn't remember if Erika had said what the baby was, a boy or a girl. For that matter, he didn't know why she'd told him the truth after all these years of silence. What did it have to do with that letter?

Steven wouldn't know the answers until he returned home. He wouldn't know until he let Erika finish her confession.

But maybe he didn't want to know.

Not now. Not ever.

Steven had crossed into Oregon before he reached the end of his rage. He pulled into a rest stop, cut the engine, and leaned his forehead against the steering wheel.

His mind replayed the years of his marriage to Erika, the highs and the lows, the ups and the downs. She was his wife, his lover, his friend, and at times, his conscience. She was the mother of his son, his encourager, his cheerleader, his inspiration. She was everything a wife was supposed to be. . . .

Except the woman he'd thought she was.

How could he forgive her for *this?* How?

Forgive, the Bible told him, and he would be forgiven. He'd never found that an onerous task. He'd never been the sort of man who held a grudge.

But *this* . . .

He didn't know if he *could* forgive this. He didn't know if he had it in him.

CHAPTER ELEVEN

AFTER STEVEN MISSED their scheduled lunch on Wednesday, Dallas called the school twice, leaving messages with the secretary. He called the Welby home three times and left messages on the answering machine. When Steven still hadn't returned his calls by that evening, Dallas started to worry. It wasn't like Steven to miss an appointment or ignore phone calls.

At nine-thirty, he called again. This time he didn't get the machine.

"Hey, Ethan," Dallas said, relieved. "Is your dad around?"

"No. Don't know where he is. I just got home from work, and his car's not in the garage. Mom's already in bed."

"Is there something going on there?"

"I wish I knew," the boy answered softly. "Mom's been acting kinda funny since Sunday, but Dad's seemed okay, if you don't count his worrying about Mom."

"Yeah, he told me yesterday that she was upset, and he didn't know why."

"Want me to have Dad call you when he gets in?"

"Please. Tell him I'll be up late so it's okay to call any time before midnight."

"If he doesn't get home soon, I'll leave him a note. Cammi and I are going out."

"Okay. Just put it where he'll be sure to see it. Thanks, Ethan."

"Sure thing. So long."

Dallas hung up the phone.

"If that frown gets any deeper," Paula said, "it's going to carve a permanent groove in your forehead."

He glanced across the kitchen. His wife stood in the patio doorway, her skin glittering with water after a swim in the pool. She looked—what did his secretary call that delivery boy this afternoon?—luscious. It wasn't a word he would normally think of, but it seemed to apply to Paula at the moment.

Paula asked, "When did you get home?"

"Just a short while ago. The meeting ran long." He walked across the kitchen and gathered her into his embrace. "Sorry for missing dinner." He nuzzled her neck.

"Oh, Dallas. You're getting your clothes wet." She gently pushed him away with the heels of her hands.

That wasn't exactly the reaction he'd been hoping for.

She stepped around him and headed for the refrigerator. "I didn't eat anything myself," she said. "I had work to go over before tomorrow. Warren Carmichael seems very interested in the proposal we presented to him. If Henry & Associates gets to develop their new business complex, we'll be up to our ears in work for the next three or four years."

"That's great," he answered, although Dallas couldn't care less about Warren Carmichael or any of her other clients, not with the way she looked in that green bathing suit.

Paula filled a glass with water, then turned to face him. "I think I'm going to turn in now. I'm beat."

"Turning in sounds like a good idea." He smiled, hoping she'd catch his drift.

Giving her head a tiny shake, she said, "Not tonight, Dallas. I really am worn out."

Getting shut down so quickly didn't put him in a good mood. "Did you call and make your doctor appointment today?"

"No." She set the glass on the counter. "I forgot."

"Come on, Paula. How can we find out about why we aren't pregnant yet if you don't go see your doctor?"

"I told you. I had a busy day. I forgot."

"Well, I had a busy day, too, but I still managed to do the things that were important to me."

"If looks could kill" was the perfect description for the glance she sent his way before she whirled and headed out of the room.

Dallas cursed. Maybe a swim would be a good idea. He needed cooling off.

⁓

It was midnight before Steven finally returned home. He'd waited until he thought Erika would be asleep. He didn't want to talk to her. Not yet. He wasn't ready yet.

Of course, he knew they *needed* to talk. Nothing would be resolved by throwing up a wall of silence and recrimination. Yes, he knew that. But he felt like a bystander at one of those deadly traffic accidents. He couldn't seem to control what was happening; he could only stand and watch helplessly.

Erika and Dallas.

The words taunted him.

Erika and Dallas together.

The images haunted him.

Has she been tempted to be with him again? Is that why she never told me?

The thoughts and images taunted and haunted him throughout the night as he lay in their bed, clinging to his side so there was no danger they might touch. When sleep still hadn't visited him by four o'clock in the morning, he got up, showered, and left early for the Thursday morning men's Bible study he'd attended for the past seven years.

Steven put on his I'm-a-good-Christian-all's-right-with-the-world face as he talked with the other men. He participated in the prayer time. He quoted Scripture. He even had the audacity to offer words of advice to a brother who was struggling in his marriage.

But as Nick Franklin gave a brief devotional, Steven's thoughts drifted, recalling the way his wife had looked on their wedding day, coming down the aisle dressed in white satin and lace. He remembered the joy of her countenance. She'd been indescribably beautiful, her pale blue eyes shining with love for him. He'd felt like the luckiest guy in the world.

At least, he'd thought she was in love with him. He'd thought himself lucky. But maybe that too had all been a lie.

Confession might have been good for the soul, but there was no way he was telling anybody from church that his wife had slept with his best friend and then given birth to an illegitimate child. No way. Many couples looked to him and Erika as an example of what a marriage should and could be.

What a crock!

❧

Kirsten wasn't surprised when she opened the door to her apartment at a quarter to eight in the morning to find her mother waiting on the other side. She'd known her mother would come by as soon as her shift at the all-night diner was over.

"You're really going through with this move, aren't you?" Donna Lundquist asked after kissing Kirsten on the cheek.

"Yes." She sighed softly. "I'm really going through with it." She held the door open wide. "Come in, Mom."

"What if you don't like living out there?" Donna's tone made it sound as if Idaho were on the moon.

"I won't know until I get there, will I?"

Her mother moved to the middle of the living room, her gaze sliding over the boxes stacked everywhere. "You won't know anyone. What if you get sick? There'll be no one to care for you. Why don't you stay and marry Van?"

"Well, for one thing, he's never asked me."

"He will if you give him time. Maybe you just need to drop a few hints, give him a little encouragement."

Kirsten sighed again. "Marriage isn't the answer to everything." She knew her mother would never accept that comment as truth. Donna Lundquist—who'd been so happily married—was a throwback to another age, believing that a woman's only way to true fulfillment was through a husband.

Donna walked toward the kitchen. "If your father were alive today, you'd think differently."

Maybe that was true. Maybe if Felix Lundquist had lived, Kirsten's life *would* have been different, better, just as her mother said. But he hadn't lived. He'd died from a massive heart attack at the age of forty-four, thrusting his widow and two-year-old adopted daughter into almost instant poverty. What little insurance he'd carried had gone for hospital bills and funeral expenses.

Donna had ended up as a waitress in a bar and grill,

the first of countless waitressing jobs she'd held over the years.

She had sacrificed in countless ways for her daughter, had done her best to give Kirsten everything she'd needed and much of what she'd wanted. But what Kirsten had wanted most was a dad, and that she'd never had.

"I'd like to make some decaf," Donna called from the kitchen. "Where's your coffeemaker?"

"It's packed."

"Which box is it in?"

Kirsten clenched her hands at her sides as she stepped into the kitchen doorway. "I don't know, Mom. You'll have to make do with instant."

"Instant coffee?" Donna made a face. "I can't stand the stuff. Never could."

"It's all I've got."

Suddenly, her mom burst into tears. "How am I going to bear it without you? You're all I have." She hid her face in her hands, her shoulders trembling. "I'll be lost without you. I'm afraid you'll never come back."

"Oh, Mom." Kirsten crossed the kitchen and put her arms around Donna, squeezing tightly. "I love you. That isn't going to change, no matter where I live. I need to do this. It's my job. And who knows. Maybe I'll get a promotion. Besides, it'll be good for me to see a little bit of the country."

Her mother met her gaze as she drew in a shaky breath. "Have you heard from her?"

Kirsten knew whom she meant. "No."

"What if you never do?"

"I'll do exactly what I'm doing now. I'll work hard at my job and live my life the best way I can. It's all any of us can do."

❧

"Mom?"

It took a moment before Erika registered her son's voice, a moment longer before she found the strength to turn her head and look at him.

"What's going on?" Ethan came into his parents' bedroom and sat on the edge of the bed next to her.

She touched his cheek with her fingertips. She remembered how smooth and soft his skin used to be. Now she could feel the stubble of his youthful beard.

"Mom? Are you and Dad . . . are you having some sort of trouble?"

She almost laughed. Almost.

"You can tell me," Ethan went on.

"I don't know if I can."

"I'm not a kid anymore."

They'd always been close, she and her son. She'd always been able to talk openly with him about so many things. Maybe it was because he was an only child.

Not really an only child. The thought pierced her heart afresh.

Erika drew a deep breath. "This is all so hard."

"You're not . . ." Ethan stiffened. "You and Dad aren't getting a divorce, are you?"

She stared at him, not knowing what to answer. She

didn't know what was going to happen. Steven wouldn't talk to her. For that matter, she hadn't seen him since he walked out of the house yesterday morning, slamming the door behind him. She knew he'd returned last night. She'd felt his presence in the bed even in her troubled sleep. But he'd left again this morning without a word.

"Tell me, Mom."

"All right," she said on a sigh. "But it won't be easy." She lowered her gaze, unable to look at him and say the things she must.

"It'll be okay, whatever it is."

Will it? I don't know. I just don't know.

She took another deep breath. "When I was sixteen . . . Well, your grandpa and I weren't close the way you are with your dad. But you know that. I felt really alone a lot of the time. Then I met your dad and fell in love. I had all kinds of girlish dreams for our future." She smiled, but it was tinged with sadness. "When Steven went off to college, I felt more alone than ever. I missed him terribly."

Ethan's expression revealed his bewilderment. He'd heard the stories of his parents' high school romance countless times, and he had to be wondering why she'd said this was difficult to talk about.

"That fall," she continued resolutely, "after your dad left for college, I went to a party where they had some of those big kegs of beer. I got pretty tipsy that night."

"*You?*"

"Yes." Erika sighed. "I did something stupid. I went home with . . . with a boy." She fell silent, and the bedroom seemed to be holding its breath. Somehow she found the courage to meet and hold her son's gaze. "Ethan, I . . . I got pregnant."

He recoiled as if she'd slapped him.

She wanted to stop. She didn't want to say more. She wanted things to go back to the way they'd been a week ago.

But she couldn't stop. That option no longer existed.

"I went away to have the baby. I gave her up for adoption. Your dad never knew about it. Neither did your grandpa." The words came tumbling out of her now, in a hurry to be done. "When your dad came back after getting his degree, he and I started dating again. I never told him what happened to me. It was my secret."

Ethan frowned. "So Dad found out about the baby. Is that it?"

"That letter I got last weekend. It was from—" her voice dropped to a whisper—"my . . . my daughter."

"Your *daughter*?" His eyes widened. "She *wrote* to you?"

Erika nodded. "Her name is Kirsten. Kirsten Lundquist. She's moving to Boise, and she wants to meet me." She took hold of his hand, clutching it between both of hers. "She's going to want to meet her father, too."

A thick silence blanketed the room before Ethan said, "Is he somebody I know?"

Erika's grip tightened, not wanting him to pull away. "Ethan, honey, it's Dallas."

He did pull away. "What're you saying?" He stood.

"We didn't mean . . . We never—"

"You and . . . and *him*!"

She could see the horror on her son's face. Dallas was like a second father to Ethan.

"That's . . . that's *sick*, Mom!"

"We made a mistake. Try to understand, honey."

He took a step back. "You and Dallas hid it from Dad all these years? How could you do that to him? How could both of you lie like that?"

It was her turn to draw back. "I'm the one who hid it." She shook her head. "Dallas doesn't know." She turned, unable to look at Ethan a moment longer. "I never told him I was pregnant."

*A*UGUST 1980

"That's it, Erika. You're doing great. One more push. Just one more."

A groan that increased to a scream was torn from her throat at the precise moment her young body pushed the new life into the world.

"It's a girl," the doctor announced.

Erika closed her eyes and turned her head to one side as the baby began to cry.

"Do you want to see her, dear?" the nurse asked.

"No," Erika whispered.

She'd been told that would be better: Don't see the baby. Just let it go. You're doing the right thing.

There's a wonderful couple waiting for a child. The baby will have a terrific life, and now so can you.

She wished Grams was with her. She longed for home, for the familiar. She missed her room, her friends, her school. She even missed her dad.

Most of all, she missed Steven.

Tears slid from beneath her eyelids.

It's over now. It's over.

In the following minutes, her body expelled the afterbirth. The nurses removed the baby from the delivery room. Erika's medical needs were attended to with crisp efficiency, and she was taken to another room on another floor, far from the maternity ward and the nursery full of babies.

It's over now. It's over.

A hospital was a place full of strange sounds and strange smells, and in the middle of a sleepless night, it seemed the loneliest place in the world to a young girl who would never meet the daughter she'd just borne.

CHAPTER Twelve

ERIKA AWAKENED from a deep sleep borne of depression and exhaustion.

Her first thought was *Call her.*

With her husband angry and her teenage son confused, Erika didn't know if she could call Kirsten, didn't know if she should.

Call her.

She sat up, not wanting to awaken Steven. He'd stayed out late again last night. When he'd returned, he'd lain in the bed beside her, his body rigid, as if afraid they might accidentally touch. As if she were . . . unclean.

She got out of bed, then more out of habit than anything, she reached for her devotional journal in the drawer of her nightstand. Beneath it was the letter. She picked it up, too.

Call her.

How could she? How could she now, with her life crumbling about her ears?

She grabbed her Bible, setting it on top of her devotional, then left the bedroom. At Ethan's closed bedroom door, she stopped and placed one hand flat against the surface, as if she could touch him through it.

I'm sorry. I never meant to disappoint you.

Ethan had shut himself in his room last night, the music on his stereo blaring away for hours.

I was young. I made a mistake. I'm sorry.

But neither Ethan nor his father seemed inclined at this point to hear her.

Erika moved down the hallway and into the family room, where she sat on the couch and switched on the nearby table lamp.

I feel alone, God.

She ran her fingers across the cover of the journal. Not long ago, within these pages, she'd begun to write about the men in her life. It had started because of a comment Barb Dobson had made.

"When I go to God in my quiet time," Barb had said, wearing a peaceful smile, "I usually begin with, 'Hi, Daddy. It's me.' Then I just bask in His presence and let Him love me for a while."

Erika had experienced a sharp stab of envy upon hearing those words. She loved God, but she'd never imagined approaching Him in such a fashion. Why not? she'd wondered.

And so she'd begun to write as a means of discovery.

Erika opened the journal, then flipped through the pages, stopping to read a few paragraphs, then turning a few more and reading again, then again and again.

Poppa Clyde, my dad's father, always reminded me of Santa Claus. He didn't have a white beard, but he had a big, soft belly and a nose that was round on the end, like a little ball.

I didn't get to see Poppa Clyde often because he lived in Oregon, but those times he came for a visit were always special. He kept those little caramel squares in his pockets and would slip them to me whenever my dad wasn't looking.

I always felt like I couldn't do any wrong in Poppa Clyde's eyes. He died when I was about six or seven. I wish I could have known him longer.

I wonder if God sees me the way Poppa Clyde did?

My father. It's hard to write about Dad because I always feel so confused. And it's sad that I feel that way at my age, I think. It isn't that I'm still afraid of him, the way I was when I was young, but I've never quite gotten over that need to please him, to make him proud of me. Just once to feel like he really, really loved me.

Do I love him? Yes, but even that's confusing. It's colored by the way he is with me.

Sometimes I remember him as being different. That was before Mom died, I guess, because she is always part of those memories, too.

Why is it that I can't seem to move on, that I
seem stuck in my teen years whenever I'm with him?
It isn't healthy. I'm sure of that, and I think it's why
I can't say, "Hi, Daddy. It's me," when I'm talking
to God.

I'm so blessed to be married to a man like Steven
and to have a son like Ethan. They mean the world
to me. When I think how different it is for wives
and mothers all over this country, I wonder why I
have been so fortunate. I really do have the perfect
family.

Erika felt those last words echo in her heart. *The
perfect family.*
Steven . . . and Ethan . . . and Kirsten.
Call her.

Kirsten awakened that morning in a cold sweat, wondering if she was making a colossal mistake. She'd ended
her relationship with Van. Her mother was heartbroken.
She'd given up her apartment. She was preparing to drive
across the country in a ten-year-old vehicle to take a job
with a modest salary in a strange city.
How much crazier could a girl get than that?
Yet she couldn't back out now. She had to go. She
had to see this through. Crazy or not, she was going.
Besides, the movers had loaded her meager belong-

ings into the van yesterday and had driven away. If she changed her mind, who knew when she might see her things again.

"Boise or bust," she muttered as she rolled up her sleeping bag.

After a quick shower, she took one last look around the empty apartment, then retrieved her keys from the front pocket of her purse and headed for the door. The ringing of the telephone stopped her.

Grabbing the handset, she said, "Hello?"

Silence.

"Hello?"

"I'm sorry. Is this . . . is this Kirsten Lundquist?"

"Yes. Who's this?" If it was a sales call at this hour, so help her, she would slam the phone in the woman's ear.

More silence.

"Listen, I was just about to—"

"It's Erika Welby."

Kirsten caught her breath.

"Is this a bad time? I can call back later if it would be more convenient."

"No, I . . . I can talk now." Kirsten tried to steady her nerves. "I guess you got my letter."

Another pause, then, "Yes."

The woman had a soft, pleasant voice. Kirsten closed her eyes, imagining what she looked like.

"It came as a . . . surprise," Erika added.

Kirsten's grasp on the phone tightened. "*Are* you my birth mother?"

"Yes, I believe I am."

Kirsten had a thousand questions to ask, and yet she couldn't speak a one.

"Are you . . . are you still moving to Boise?"

"Yes. I'm leaving today."

"When does your flight arrive?"

"I'm driving."

"Alone?"

"Yes. It's just me."

"I see." Another silence.

Do you care who I am? Will you tell me who my father is?

As if reading Kirsten's thoughts, Erika said, "I don't know when we'll be able to meet."

Kirsten heard the unspoken qualifier: *Or if we'll be able to.*

"Things are . . . they're rather complicated right now."

"I see." Kirsten hoped she'd kept her disappointment out of those two simple words.

"I . . . I'll call you after you've had time to get settled."

Will you? Kirsten wondered.

"I'll call you in a few weeks," Erika said. "That's the best way, I think. For you to wait for me to call you after you've had a chance to get settled."

She didn't think Erika Welby sounded too sure.

"I won't keep you any longer, Kirsten. I hope you have a . . . a safe trip."

"Thanks. I will."

"Well . . . good-bye, then."

"Bye."

Click.

Bzzzz.

Kirsten listened to the dial tone for thirty seconds before hanging up.

⌇

Steven stood in the hallway, hidden in the shadows, listening. Eavesdropping and hating himself for it.

He stepped into the kitchen. Erika turned from the wall phone, as if sensing his presence.

"You called her," he said.

"Yes."

Steven moved toward the table. "How'd she sound?"

"Nervous. Same as me."

Her reply set his teeth on edge.

"Steven?"

"What?"

"Maybe we should see a marriage counselor."

"We don't need a counselor." He stuffed his fingertips in the pockets of his jeans. "We need time. *I* need time."

"Ethan's upset."

His heart sank. "You told him, didn't you?"

"I didn't have a choice."

"We *always* have choices, Erika."

"He's scared about what's happening to us. He needed to—"

"And that's *my* fault? *I'm* not the one who slept around. *My* only child is legitimate." His words were cruel, and their harshness took him as much by surprise as they did Erika.

She grew visibly pale as she stared at him, eyes wide, mouth slightly parted.

If he'd hated himself for eavesdropping, he despised himself even more for this. Yet he couldn't take back the hateful words. They'd been spoken into existence, and he could never take them back.

Erika clenched her hands together at her waist. "What is it you want from me, Steven?"

What he wanted was to apologize. What he said was, "I don't know."

Without a word, tears in her eyes, Erika left the kitchen.

"What is it you want from me, Steven?"

He sat down.

"What is it you want?"

"I don't know," he whispered. "I really don't know."

Moving by instinct rather than design, Erika took Motley's leash from the nail just inside the garage door, snapped it onto the dog's collar, then left with him through the gate on the west side of the house.

She tried to pray but her thoughts were too unfocused, her heart in too much pain. So she walked.

The neighborhood was like an old friend to her, comfortable, familiar. The Welby family had lived on this street for the past fifteen years. Their subdivision had been built in the fifties, and their neighbors were made up of elderly retirees, young couples starting out, and every kind of home owner in between.

Ethan had grown up here. He'd learned to ride his bike on these sidewalks. He'd broken his left ankle while trying to jump over Mrs. Freckleton's hedge on a dare.

As a stay-at-home mom, Erika had volunteered to help at her son's schools, first elementary, then junior high, and finally high school. She'd liked those early years the most, of course. That was when she could walk to school, holding her son's hand. Those days ended when Ethan entered the seventh grade. At that point, she'd been forbidden to kiss him in public and requested not to make a scene should their paths cross in the school hallways.

She wondered if Kirsten's adoptive mother had volunteered at her schools. Had Kirsten been a happy child? Had she learned to ride her bike on a street similar to this one? Had she broken a bone or cut her chin? Had an insensitive boy ever broken her schoolgirl's heart?

Erika felt a wave of sadness wash over her, a sense of all the moments she'd missed, all the memories she'd lost when she signed away her baby girl to be raised by strangers. But if she'd kept Kirsten, would she have lost Steven forever? Would Ethan have been born? Would Kirsten have suffered if Erika's decision had been to keep her? Or had she suffered because Erika chose to give her away?

She would never have answers to those questions. She couldn't know what might have been any more than she could know the future.

And oh, how she wished she knew the future.

Most of all, she wished she could foresee Steven's forgiveness.

"I'm not the one who slept around. My only child is legitimate."

She winced as she recalled the venom in her husband's voice. Steven had never spoken to her like that. He'd never been intentionally cruel. He was hurting. She understood that. He felt betrayed, and she couldn't blame him. But would he be able to forgive her? If not today, tomorrow or the next day or the next? And if he didn't, what was to become of them?

CHAPTER THIRTEEN

STEVEN COULDN'T STAND the accusing silence of the house. So he tossed his clubs into the trunk of his car and headed for the golf course. It was one of the advantages of his job, having more time off in the summer than the average working stiff. He wouldn't have a problem getting a spur-of-the-moment tee time on a Friday morning.

Clover Creek was an eighteen-hole public golf course. Nothing fancy, but it was well maintained and the people were friendly. In addition, the rates were reasonable, befitting the budget of an elementary school principal.

Dallas preferred to play at the exclusive Desert Heights Country Club.

Dallas.

With his mood growing more foul by the second, Steven whipped into the Clover Creek parking lot. He slid into an open space and cut the engine. It only took him a few minutes to put on his golf shoes, grab his clubs from the trunk, and head inside to arrange for a tee time. Fortunately, they weren't busy. Nobody tried to pair him up with another player. He was thankful for that. The last thing he wanted was to make idle conversation with a stranger.

By the eighth hole, he'd lost six balls, two in the neighboring cornfields and four in the course's ponds and streams. Adding insult to injury, he was ten strokes over par. Maybe playing golf wasn't the best way to improve his mood.

He thought things couldn't get worse.

He was wrong.

Dallas was waiting for him at the tenth hole.

"What are you doing here?" Steven asked when he realized who it was standing near the tee box.

"I stopped by your house. Erika said you'd left while she was out and your clubs were gone." Dallas shrugged. "Two and two made four."

Steven said nothing.

"What's going on, Steve? You missed our lunch, and you haven't returned any of my calls."

Steven yanked his driver from the bag. "I came here to golf, not talk."

"Fair enough." Dallas tossed a golf ball into the air, caught it, then said, "I'll play the back nine with you."

"I'd rather play alone." He jammed the tee into the earth. "If you don't mind."

"Well, yeah, I guess I do mind. I paid my fee already."

Steven gripped the driver with both hands. "Suit yourself." He positioned himself, peered toward the flag above the tenth hole, then pulled back the club and swung for all he was worth. The ball sailed through the air, straight toward the green.

Dallas let out a low whistle. "You've been practicing, buddy."

It was all Steven could do not to swing his driver at Dallas's head. Instead, he shoved the club into the bag and took off down the blacktop path, not waiting to watch Dallas tee off, not even caring at this point if he got nailed by a flying golf ball.

Dallas allowed Steven his silence for three holes before making another attempt at conversation, just as they reached the thirteenth green.

"Steve, this is crazy. You're mad about something. It would help if I knew what, so spit it out."

"Let it go, Dallas."

"I don't think so. Erika looks like she's been dragged through a knothole backwards."

Steven strode up to Dallas, almost nose to nose. "What my wife looks like is *my* business. It's not any of yours."

"Hey!" Dallas raised his hands in a sign of surrender. "Cool off. I'm just trying to help."

"Help?" Steven took a swing at him with his fist but missed.

"Whoa, buddy. What the—"

Steven swung again, this time clipping Dallas's chin before he could get out of the way.

Dallas stared at him, his face flushed, his eyes angry, while he rubbed his jaw.

Steven glared back, hating his friend, hating himself.

"I don't know what I did to deserve that, but I guess I did something."

"Oh, you did," Steven said. "Trust me, you did plenty."

"All I can say is, it's a good thing I'm not a Christian. I'd have to turn the other cheek, and I'm not sure I could do that." He reached for his golf bag. "Guess golf wasn't a good idea after all. Call me when you're ready to talk."

Steven took a step backward. "I suggest you talk to Erika." He grabbed his own golf bag and strode away.

Dallas's words followed him, ringing in his ears: "*Good thing I'm not a Christian.*" The indictment was well deserved. Steven's behavior had been anything but Christlike. Not toward Dallas and certainly not toward Erika.

But right this minute, he didn't care.

❧

Dallas decided to take Steven's advice. He drove to the Welby home to talk to Erika.

He got out of his car and walked to the front door with determined steps. He rang the bell, then waited impatiently for it to be answered.

Erika opened the door. For an instant, he caught a glimpse of hope in her eyes. Then it disappeared.

Man, something was really wrong here, and whatever it was, Dallas meant to get to the bottom of it.

"I saw Steven at the golf course," he said. "He told me you and I need to talk."

She stared at him a moment or two, then nodded, a look of resignation on her face as she let him in. He walked past her, stopped, turned, and waited.

"O God," she whispered, "please."

He felt a sudden irritation. "Come on, Erika. Is this so bad you've got to pray first?"

"Yes." She looked at him. "It is." She led the way into the living room.

Unnerved by her reply, Dallas took a seat.

Erika gave her head a slight shake. "You're the third person I've had to tell this story to. You'd think it would get easier, but it doesn't." Her voice dropped slightly. "In fact, I think it gets harder."

He wondered if Erika and Steven were getting a divorce. They would be the last couple he'd expect it from, but stranger things happened. As crazy as Steven had acted today, he figured it was a possibility.

"Dallas, do you remember your first year in college?"

He raised an eyebrow, thinking it an odd question in the middle of a serious discussion. "For the most part," he answered.

"Do you remember what happened . . . between us?"

He stiffened. It wasn't a memory he cared to dredge up.

"There's something I've kept from you," Erika continued. "I . . . I got pregnant."

"You *what?*" He was on his feet.

"I gave her up for adoption at birth."

"Her?"

There were tears in Erika's eyes. "Your . . . daughter."

My daughter? He got up, turned his back, then walked to the opposite side of the room, trying to make sense of it. A chill shot through him as he rubbed the sore spot on his jaw. He turned slowly to face her. "You told *Steve?*"

She nodded. "I had to."

"But *why?*"

"She wrote to me." Erika wiped the tears from her cheeks with her fingertips. "She's coming to Boise to live. She wants to meet me." She paused a heartbeat, then said, "And she'll want to meet you, too."

Dallas's silence seemed worse than anything he could say.

Why aren't you with me, Steven? Why aren't we telling Dallas together?

Throughout her adult life, her husband had been beside her in times of crisis. But not this time. This time, he'd left her to face everything alone.

Will he ever be beside me again?

"When?" Dallas asked.

Erika blinked, surprised by the sound of his voice. "When what?"

"When is the girl coming to Boise?"

She drew a shaky breath. "She's on her way now, I think."

He rubbed his forehead with the fingers of one hand. "Not much warning."

112

"No."

"What if I don't want anything to do with her?"

"That'll be up to you. She doesn't know your name."

He turned toward the window. "Paula isn't going to like this news."

"I'm sorry," she whispered. "I can't do anything about that."

"Look, I . . . I'd better go. I need to figure this out."

"Of course." She stood. "I understand."

She didn't bother to follow him to the door. Instead, she sank listlessly onto the sofa.

Time passed, but she had no concept of how much or how little it was before she heard the garage door open. She tensed. Each minute dragged by as she waited to hear her husband enter the house. When Steven stepped into the living-room entry, Erika felt a sharp pain in her chest. He looked beaten, defeated, and it made her want to cry again. Steven had always been strong, but he didn't look strong now.

Their gazes locked. She held her breath, waiting.

At last, he said, "Dallas came to the golf course."

"I know." She swallowed hard. "He came here after seeing you."

"Did he tell you what happened?"

"He said you told him to talk to me."

Steven stepped into the room, glancing at his right hand. "I hit him," he said softly as he formed a fist.

So, her lie had brought him to this. Her vision blurred, but she kept the tears from falling. "I'm sorry. I'm so sorry, Steven."

Wordlessly, he sat in the chair.

She wondered if the friendship between the two men was irrevocably broken. She longed to go to him but she didn't move.

"I've never felt that kind of rage before," Steven said, more to himself than to her.

"It's understandable."

"Is it?" He shook his head.

O God, what do I say to him? What can I do to make things better? She said the only thing she could: "I love you, Steven."

He rubbed his knuckles. "I don't know where to go from here, what to do next." He stared at the floor, midway between where he sat and where she sat.

Tell me you love me, Steven. That's where we should begin. Hold me. Take my hand or put your arm around my shoulders. Touch me in some way. Any way.

But Steven couldn't hear her thoughts, and he didn't come to hold her as she desired.

⁂

Kirsten dropped onto the bed in the small motel in North Olmstead, Ohio.

Four hundred and forty miles down. Two thousand thirty miles to go.

The motel wasn't exactly a four-star establishment. Even a three would be generous. But it looked clean, and it was a good distance from the interstate so the constant noise of semis on the freeway wouldn't keep her awake. Most importantly, it fit her budget.

Kirsten groaned, then made herself rise and go into the bathroom, where she brushed her teeth and washed her face. She undressed, tossing her clothes across a chair before slipping into a nightshirt. Minutes later, she returned to the bed, this time pulling back the spread, blanket, and top sheet and climbing in.

But she didn't fall instantly asleep as she'd expected she would. Instead, her thoughts flitted from one thing to another.

Four hundred and forty miles from Philly. That was farther from home than she'd ever traveled.

Although she was born in Boston, the Lundquist family had moved to Philadelphia before Kirsten's second birthday, and that was where she and her mother had stayed after the death of Felix Lundquist. Kirsten's mother had struggled to make ends meet, week to week, month to month, year to year. There hadn't been money for trips to Disney World or other vacation spots. Kirsten hadn't even made it to New York City until she graduated from high school, and then it had happened only with the help of her closest girlfriends.

Now she was moving clear across the country. She was driving alone in an older model Toyota to a state she knew little about.

I must be insane.

But if she didn't go, she wouldn't meet Erika Welby. And if she didn't meet Erika, she would never learn the facts of her birth or discover who her father was.

She closed her eyes and tried to imagine him. He hadn't been identified on her original birth certificate; he remained nameless. Perhaps Erika didn't know where he was. Or even *who* he was.

Kirsten didn't like to entertain that notion. She wanted her dad to be someone special. How often had she looked in the mirror and tried to envision him? Was his hair black and curly like hers? Did he have the same olive complexion or the same dimples? Were his eyes brown like hers?

Whatever he looked like, Kirsten was certain he must be kind and caring. He *must* be.

It was foolish, of course, to romanticize the stranger who'd sired her, but she couldn't help it. Sometimes she imagined he'd been searching for her all these years. When she was little, she liked to pretend he would arrive one day at her school and whisk her away to a castle somewhere.

"Princess Kirsten," she whispered, mocking herself.

Lights flashed against the curtains as a vehicle pulled into the parking space outside her room. Car doors opened, then slammed closed. A young boy's voice rose in complaint. A father's rebuke silenced him. A mother's softer words offered comfort.

Strangers, traveling the freeway, the same as Kirsten. Only they were a family. A *real* family. Where were they going? As far as she? No, probably not that far.

She rolled onto her side, turning her back toward the window of the motel room.

Five more days of travel, two thousand and some miles, and she would be in Boise.

In recent weeks, Kirsten had spent hours on the

Internet, studying the pages at www.cityofboise.org and other related sites. She'd looked at the photos of the mountains and the river, the city skyline by day and by night, the zoo and the parks. She'd studied the street maps, figuring out the best route from her apartment— arranged for, sight unseen, through a rental agency—to her new office.

Even with all her research, she knew her world would be turned upside down for a long time to come. Everything would feel strange because it wouldn't be home, because she would be alone.

But if she could find her dad and if he could love her, even a little . . .

Tears slipped from the corners of her eyes, dampening her pillow.

I want it so much. So very, very much.

CHAPTER FOURTEEN

"WHAT'S GOING ON?"

Dallas glanced up from the sports page of the paper.

Paula gave him a disgusted look. "You didn't hear a word I said at supper last night, and you're doing the same thing this morning. What's on your mind?"

Tell her about the girl, a small voice prompted.

Ironic, wasn't it? He'd wondered if there was something wrong with him in the fatherhood department, and it turned out he'd been one for—what?—nearly twenty-two years. Of course, Steven would say it took more than impregnation to make a man a father.

Steven . . .

Frowning, Dallas rubbed his jaw.

"Are you listening to me?" Paula demanded.

"I'm sorry." He folded the paper, then set it aside. "I was thinking about Steve . . . and Erika."

"What about them?"

Tell her.

Yesterday, Steven had punched him in anger. That was probably nothing compared to what Paula would do when she found out about his fling with Erika all those years ago.

"Well?" Paula said.

"They . . . they're having problems. I'm worried about them."

"What kind of problems?" She sat down opposite him. "You mean in their marriage?"

"Yes."

"So, spill the details, Dallas. Don't leave me hanging."

"I don't know much." That was a lie, but he didn't care. He was telling her that his best friend's marriage was in trouble, and all she wanted were the gory details. He could see it in her eyes. She wanted the gossip.

She gave him a knowing smile as she rose slowly from her chair and came around the table. Draping her arms around his neck, she whispered, "Ve have vays to make you talk."

This was supposed to be the moment when he willingly rose from his chair and cradled his wife in his arms. This was supposed to be the moment when he told her whatever she wanted to hear. That was how it had worked before. But this time was different. This time her attempts to entice only served to irritate.

Did she really not care about their friends?

He lightly grasped her upper arms and held her away from him. "Not now, Paula."

She stiffened, and the surprise in her green eyes was almost comical. Only he found no humor in it.

Paula's surprise was followed by a glimmer of anger and then by something not so easily defined.

"Okay," she said softly. "I understand." She gave him a tender smile. "I can see you're worried." Leaning forward, she brushed her lips against his forehead. "Maybe I should share some good news." She slipped off his lap, standing near his chair, the fingers of her right hand resting on his chest. "I called my gynecologist. They were able to squeeze me in next week. I told them I needed to begin fertility tests."

He glanced up.

"I want a baby every bit as much as you do, Dallas. I'm sorry we've fought over this."

Looking at her, he was reminded of the night they met. They'd been at a political fund-raiser, both of them with other dates. Paula had bumped into him on the dance floor. He'd taken one look at the petite, green-eyed, red-haired beauty—all of twenty years old at the time—and he'd known he was a goner.

They were a lot alike, he and his wife. They were ambitious, driven, success-oriented. Neither was afraid of hard work or long hours in order to get what they each wanted. And they had just about everything. They lived the good life. And yet Dallas felt somehow hollow. For a long time he'd thought the only thing they needed to make the picture perfect was a child.

But was that true?

Suddenly, he wasn't so sure. Suddenly, he wondered whether that hollow feeling inside him could be filled even by a baby.

↷

Ethan ate breakfast and left for his job at the hardware store. Steven announced that he had yard work to do before the day got too warm.

With both of her men out of the house and the radio tuned to an oldies station, Erika put the breakfast dishes in the dishwasher, then wiped down the kitchen counters. Next, she changed the sheets on the beds and put the dirty linens in the washing machine. It was a familiar Saturday morning routine, one Erika could probably do while sleepwalking.

She was on the way to retrieve the vacuum cleaner from the hall closet when her mind betrayed her.

Where's Kirsten now? How far across the country did she come yesterday?

Erika stopped, then turned and walked into the living room. She gazed around, as if she'd never seen the room before, not certain what she'd come here for. Finally, she sat on the nearest chair.

It isn't safe for a young woman to drive so far alone. Why didn't I object?

Because she had no right to object. She'd given away that right when she'd put her baby up for adoption.

What could I have done differently?

She was tired of that question. She was tired of self-recriminations.

She rose again, restless, unsettled. She walked to the window and stared at the front lawn, a deep emerald green, still damp from the sprinklers.

Did Kirsten grow up in a house with a front yard? Or was her home an apartment in the city?

Odd, how Erika had been able to keep thoughts of this child—her firstborn—from her mind through the years, and now she could think of little else.

What if I don't like her? What if she doesn't like me?

Dreadful possibilities, but possibilities all the same.

She closed her eyes and remembered Ethan as a baby, as a toddler, as a five-year-old learning to ride his bike, as a young boy going off to school for the first time.

So many memories of her son, and not even one of her daughter. Erika hadn't held Kirsten after giving birth. She'd been emptied of the life she'd carried within her teenaged body, and then she'd sent the baby away.

O God, what a mess we make of things when we don't live godly lives, when we make sinful choices.

The ringing of the telephone yanked her from her thoughts. She went to answer it. "Hello?" Erika said.

"Morning, Erika."

Her throat narrowed. "Hi, Paula."

"How are you?" Her voice sounded unusually kind.

Did Paula know? Had Dallas told her?

"Fine, thanks," Erika answered with fake calm. "And you?"

"I'm terrific. Listen, I was wondering if you and

Steven could come over for supper tonight. We'll barbecue, then relax by the pool."

Erika's grip tightened around the handset. *Dallas
hasn't told her.*

"What do you say? Nothing fancy, and you don't
have to bring a thing but your swimsuits and yourselves."

"I'll have to check with Steven before I say yes or
no. Can I call you back in about an hour?"

"Of course. I've got a few errands to run this morning, so if I'm not here, leave a message."

"All right."

"Bye."

Erika placed the phone in its cradle, noticing the
slight unsteadiness of her own hand.

O God, how do You redeem a mess like this?

A scene from *Gone With the Wind* popped into her
head, the one when Scarlett walked into a party unes-
corted, wearing a dress as scarlet as her name, a party
where everyone was whispering about her, judging her,
condemning her.

"I know exactly how she felt."

~

Kirsten stopped for a late lunch at a truck stop outside of
South Bend, Indiana.

"You look beat, sweetie pie," the waitress said as
Kirsten slid into a booth. She was a plump woman, probably in her sixties, with hair dyed carrot red and a pair of
fluorescent-framed glasses perched on the tip of her

nose. Her name badge identified her as Mildred. "How 'bout some coffee? This stuff's strong enough to remove rust from the underside of a semi. It'll open those eyes of yours." She didn't wait for an answer before filling the white mug on the table.

"Thanks."

"Don't mention it." She popped her gum as she dropped a menu in front of Kirsten. "I'll be back in a jiff for your order."

Kirsten stared at the choices listed on the plastic-covered menu. The food was reasonably priced and, no doubt, trucker-sized in portions. Kirsten felt hungry enough to eat a side of beef, but she knew too big a meal would make her want to nap. She was plenty tired without that.

"You decide?" Mildred asked when she returned a few minutes later.

"Yes. I'd like the BLT on toast, please, and a cup of your soup of the day."

"Anything besides coffee to drink?"

"Just water."

Mildred took the menu. "I'll have it right out to you, hon."

Kirsten offered a weak smile. "Which way to the rest room?"

The waitress motioned with her head. "Over that away."

"Thanks."

When Mildred was gone, Kirsten pushed herself out of the booth. The truck stop was large—part restaurant, part convenience store, part video arcade. Kirsten wound her way through several aisles, looking at the shelves of food, first-aid items, and cheap bric-a-brac in the touristy section of the store.

It reminded her of her mom. Donna Lundquist had a taste for kitsch. Their apartment had been filled with trinkets and nicknacks that served no purpose except to gather dust.

For some reason, as Kirsten stared at a dashboard hula girl, she remembered the time her mom had bought a kite and they'd gone to the park to fly it. It had been one of those picture-perfect days when the sky was powder blue with a few tufts of white clouds added for texture. The trees had been thick with green leaves, their branches stirring in a gentle but steady breeze. It had taken the two of them forever to get that kite airborne. They'd been silly with giggles, the both of them, before they'd succeeded.

Homesickness washed over her. If Kirsten could have seen her mom right then, she'd gladly buy her every kitschy item in this place.

࿇

Steven listened as Erika relayed Paula's invitation, then said, "We're not going. Make up some excuse."

"I don't think Dallas has told her."

"Can't say as I blame him." He turned toward the lawn mower, wiped perspiration from his brow with his forearm, and leaned down to pull the starter.

"Steven?"

He cast an impatient glance over his shoulder without letting go of the cord.

She gave her head a slight shake. "Never mind." She turned and walked toward the house.

Steven ground his teeth in frustration. What did she want from him? All he needed was some time to work this through. Was that so much to ask?

He pulled the starter, and the mower's engine roared to life.

Maybe. Maybe not.

He was rotten through and through, Steven realized. No denying it. He couldn't make himself do right, even when he wanted to, and when he tried not to do wrong, he did it anyway.

"God, I don't understand why You've let this happen to us," he muttered.

CHAPTER FIFTEEN

I NEVER SHOULD'VE DONE THIS. I must be nuts.

The journey between Grand Island, Nebraska, and Laramie, Wyoming, yesterday had seemed long and tedious. But today had been ten times worse.

Kirsten had left all visible signs of civilization behind a thousand miles ago. The last "city" she'd passed through was Omaha. She'd even begun to long for the sight of cornfields and a silo or two, things she'd found herself cursing after several hours in Iowa. But cornfields and silos, in her humble opinion, were vastly superior to endless miles of sagebrush and nothing else.

It was day number five of her journey west, and she was two thousand twenty-nine miles from home. She missed Van and wondered if she should have convinced him to propose; they could have married, settled down, started a family of their own. She missed her mom and wished she could tell her so in person. She missed her cramped apartment with the bathroom faucet that leaked and the paper-thin walls that let her hear her neighbors when they quarreled. She missed her coworkers at Maguire & Son, including—well, almost—the smarmy maintenance guy who lurked around outside the ladies' rest room, hoping to get a date. She even missed the rush-hour traffic of Philadelphia, as hard as that was to believe.

What in the name of heaven had made her think that finding her father would be worth living in country like this?

Oh, please, don't let Boise be like this!

Kirsten's one consolation was knowing she could legally drive seventy-five miles per hour through this godforsaken wilderness. She would have gone faster, but her car's four-cylinder engine wasn't cut out for more speed.

She filled the gas tank at Little America, Wyoming, along with about thirty truckers. In the restaurant, she bolted down a greasy hamburger, some thick French fries smothered in ketchup, and a root beer while studying the road map. She wanted to reach a place called Burley before calling it a night, but that was still nearly three hundred and fifty miles away.

She made some quick calculations. Four and a half hours of driving. With luck and no head wind to buck, she'd be there by seven-thirty.

She groaned softly.

I've made an awful mistake.

～

"Bill," Dallas said into the telephone handset, "the world you and I grew up in is dead. We either move our companies into the future using every means at our disposal or we die, too."

On the other end of the line, Bill Cannon concurred. A few moments later, the conversation drew to a close.

Dallas had barely set the phone in its cradle when his secretary buzzed him.

"Mr. Welby's here to see you," Karla announced.

Dallas felt the muscles in his neck and shoulders tense. He considered telling Karla he couldn't be disturbed, but curiosity won out. "Send him in."

He stood with his back to the large plate-glass windows that lined the eastern wall of his office, the morning sunshine streaming into the room.

The door opened, and Steven entered.

"Steve."

"Dallas." Steven closed the door behind him, then stepped to the center of the office. "Sorry for showing up without calling first."

Dallas shrugged.

"I . . . owe you an apology." Steven touched his jaw, then motioned toward Dallas. "For hitting you. I shouldn't have done it. There's never a good reason for violence."

He cleared his throat. "I should've turned the other cheek. Like you said."

Steven glanced from Dallas to the window as if searching for what he wanted to say next. Dallas didn't rush him. As a businessman, he'd learned the art of appearing patient, even when he wasn't.

"I'd be lying if I said I wasn't still angry at you," Steven continued at last. "And with Erika." His eyes narrowed slightly as his gaze returned to Dallas. "You should have told me a long time ago what happened between the two of you."

"Your anger's understandable." Dallas figured he could be magnanimous now that Steven had apologized. "If I were in your shoes, I'd want to bust a few heads myself."

The corners of Steven's mouth looked pinched. He dropped his eyes.

"Do you want to sit down?" Dallas asked.

"No. I've said what I came to say."

"But—"

Steven raised a hand to stop his objection. "This isn't over, Dallas, and it's not going to be solved with an 'I'm sorry' or two. Trust's been broken." He took his raised hand and rubbed the palm over his face. "And like it or not, your daughter's arriving in Boise soon. We're all going to have to deal with the situation . . . and with her . . . for the rest of our lives."

Dallas couldn't say he cared for the sound of that. The girl was a stranger. What right had she to complicate his life this way? If she'd never written that letter . . .

Dallas turned to stare out the window. "Will you and Erika make it through this?" he asked.

"I hope so. With God's help."

Dallas thought of Paula. It didn't take an Einstein to figure out what *her* reaction would be when he worked up the nerve to tell her. "Maybe I could use a bit of that help myself."

"You probably could," Steven answered. A few moments later, he left without bothering to say good-bye.

"With God's help . . ."

Dallas had always believed in helping himself. If he wanted something done and done right, he did it. That was how he'd gotten where he was today.

And where exactly was that? he wondered. Afraid to tell his wife about some girl who claimed to be his daughter?

He grunted. He didn't see how any god could help him with Paula. She had a temper to match her fiery red hair.

And what about Steven and Erika? Was their God going to help them salvage their marriage?

He frowned, suddenly wondering if his friend had ever cheated on Erika in the years they'd been married. No, probably not. Since they'd gotten mixed up with that church a decade or so ago, they'd walked the straight and narrow. Steven didn't cuss, drink, or smoke, let alone play around on his wife.

He thought of his own marriage again. He'd come plenty close to cheating on Paula—more than once, if he was honest with himself—and it had been circumstances that kept him from following through with the inclination more than any decision in favor of fidelity.

Why was that?

He gave his head a small shake, as if to clear it. He needed to tell Paula about Kirsten, and he didn't need God's help—or anybody else's—to do it.

He stepped to his desk and punched his secretary's extension on the phone. "Karla, reschedule this afternoon's meeting with the development team to tomorrow morning. Then call the Table Top and make a dinner reservation for two at six-thirty tonight."

꒱

Lost deep in thought after leaving Dallas's office, Steven wasn't certain how he ended up on the highway that overlooked Lucky Peak Reservoir. But suddenly, there he was. He supposed he should be grateful he hadn't caused a traffic accident since he hadn't been paying attention to the road.

Up ahead, he recognized the turnoff to the old swimming cove. Without a second thought, he flipped on his signal and pressed down on the brake, then negotiated the hairpin turn off the highway. The wheels kicked up a cloud of dust as they left asphalt and hit dirt and gravel.

It had been years since he'd driven down this road, but it seemed like only yesterday. It was familiar, a part of his youth imprinted indelibly in his mind. The three of them had come here all the time.

The three of them.

Steven, Erika, and Dallas.

Arriving at the end of the road, he stopped the car, shoved it into park, and cut the engine.

Steven, Erika, and Dallas.

Steven and Erika.

Erika and Dallas.

He opened the car door and got out, then followed the footpath to the water. The floating docks were still there, looking weathered and sun bleached. Water lapped against the shore, stirred by a boat that had moved along the main channel of the reservoir half a minute before.

Steven sank onto the ground, not caring if his trousers got dirty. Not caring about much of anything these days.

Erika and Dallas.

It had meant nothing to them, their time together, or so they'd both insisted. But it meant plenty to Steven.

How often had the three of them lain upon one of those docks, baking in the hot summer sun? How often had Dallas helped Erika as she learned to come out of the water on one ski instead of two, holding her by the waist to steady her while Steven drove the boat?

Was it then, as Dallas helped her, that the seeds of their affair had been born?

He closed his eyes, his jaw clenched so tight his head hurt.

He'd told Dallas that he and Erika would make it with God's help. Only he hadn't asked for help. Not really. He felt far from God, cut adrift from his faith.

He'd asked Dallas to forgive him for striking out, but he hadn't done any forgiving in return. He couldn't.

He opened his eyes again, glaring up at the sun.

"I can't!" he shouted. "Don't ask me to!"

※

The restaurant wasn't crowded on that Tuesday evening, for which Dallas was thankful. Just enough people to make their dinner public. Not so many to make it too noisy for a serious conversation.

The perfect place and time to tell Paula about Erika . . . and a young woman named Kirsten.

They talked about business during supper, Dallas sharing his thoughts on a possible buyout of a technology firm in California, Paula revealing plans for a second phase of development in one of Henry & Associates' gated subdivisions.

It wasn't until they'd finished their dessert—cherries jubilee, Paula's favorite—that Dallas broached the difficult topic. "Paula, I've got a confession to make."

Her eyes widened slightly.

"I had an ulterior motive in bringing you here."

"If this is about me seeing the doctor, I told you I've made an—"

"It isn't about that."

She stopped, uncertainty in her gaze. "Oh."

He reached across the white tablecloth, placing his hand over hers. He forced himself to maintain eye contact, despite his inclination to look away. "It's kind of complicated, and I'm not sure how to begin."

She worried her lower lip.

Dallas took a deep breath, then plunged forward. "I told you Erika and Steve are having some problems. Well, part of it's because she kept a secret from him for a lot of years." He tightened his grip on her hand. "I need you to know that I didn't have a clue about any of this. I would have said something long before now if I had."

"You look grim. What is it?"

"Years ago, when I was a college freshman, something happened between Erika and me."

"Something? What do you mean by *something*, Dallas? Are you telling me that you and she . . . . ?" Paula let her voice trail into silence.

"Yes."

She pulled her hand from beneath his and planted it firmly in her lap. Her entire body stiffened as she waited for him to continue.

Dallas leaned back in his chair. "It wasn't an affair. It was booze and a couple of lusty kids. That's all it was, and it didn't last. It wasn't long before we couldn't stand to be around each other. Next thing I knew, she went off to school back East somewhere. I didn't see or hear about her for years. Not until after Steve got his degree and came back to Boise. He started dating Erika again, then they got married."

"Did Steven know about you two?"

"No."

"But he does now?"

Dallas nodded.

"That's why you're telling me this? Because Steven found out?"

"Yes."

"You and she aren't—"

"No!"

She visibly relaxed. "Well, then, I guess I can live with it. That was all such a long time ago."

"There's more."

"More?"

"Erika got pregnant. She had a baby girl that she gave up for adoption."

"*Your* baby?"

He nodded again. "I didn't know, Paula. She never told me. She's kept it a secret from everybody all these years. Until last week." Now he looked away, turning his gaze toward the windows overlooking the city from the fifteenth floor of the building. "The girl did a search and found Erika and wrote to her. Now she's coming here to work or live or something. That's why Erika finally told Steve the truth. And then she told me."

"Dallas, if you were a college freshman when this happened, the girl must be . . . she must be nearly as old as *I* am!"

He felt himself aging right before his wife's eyes. "Well, not quite. I think Erika said she'll be twenty-two come August."

Paula was thirty.

Sometimes eight years' age difference was too much. Sometimes it wasn't enough.

CHAPTER SIXTEEN

LYING IN BED, Erika felt Steven reach over and turn off his alarm before it could ring. But he didn't rise immediately.

"Steven." Her heart hammered in her chest as she rolled onto her side. "Steven, can't we talk about what's happening?"

He didn't answer.

"Please."

She touched his shoulder. He jerked away as if scalded, then sat up on his side of the bed.

"I've got to get ready to go," he said in a low, gravelly voice. "It's Thursday. I don't want to be late for men's group."

She felt desperate. She needed to make him talk to her, *look* at her. "What is it that bothers you the most,

Steven?" She sat up, too. "That I made a foolish mistake when I was sixteen? That I wasn't a virgin when you married me? That I gave up a baby for adoption? That I kept her a secret? What?"

He stood. "Let it be." He headed for the bathroom.

"Steven, I'm your wife. I love you." She got out of bed. *"Talk* to me."

He turned around, looking at her in the gray light of their room. "I'm not ready to talk. You had all these years to think about your little secret, but I've only had eleven days. I'm doing the best I can. So let it be. Okay? Just let it be."

She raised a beseeching hand. "I never meant to hurt you. I . . . I didn't tell you because . . . because telling you would have damaged your friendship with Dallas. I loved you too much to do that." She took a deep breath. "And I didn't tell you because I didn't want to lose you once you came back into my life. After we were married, it didn't seem important. It seemed like it happened to someone else. We were different. We were *both* different. And . . . and after I became a Christian, I asked God to forgive me." She choked back a sob. "And He did."

He glared at her a moment longer, then without a word, went into the bathroom and firmly closed the door.

"God forgave me, Steven," she whispered. "Why can't you?"

Blinded by her tears, Erika slipped into her robe, then picked up her Bible and journal and left the bedroom. She didn't stop in the kitchen to make coffee.

Instead, she went out onto the patio. She needed to feel the bracing coolness of morning on her cheeks.

Sinking onto a chair, she prayed, *God, what more can I do?*

Above the tops of the trees, a smattering of clouds in the east were stained orange and red. Birds welcomed the coming of day with chirps and whistles. In her normal world, Erika would have joined them in their songs of praise to the Creator.

But she no longer had a normal world.

NOVEMBER 1984

A bouquet of mixed flowers, purchased at the grocery store, blossomed in a vase in the center of the small round table. Two places had been set— white plates with blue trim that had been a wedding gift; silverware that had come free with the purchase of a slow cooker; some crystal stemware purchased last summer at a secondhand store; and some blue linen napkins, held snugly within white porcelain rings that had belonged to Erika's mother. Vince Gill crooned softly on the living-room stereo while the scent of baking bread wafted through the apartment.

Perfect, Erika thought.

She glanced at the clock on the wall, and her

heart skittered. Steven would be home any minute.

She dashed into the bathroom to check her hair and makeup. When she saw her reflection in the mirror, she smiled. Looking back at her was the happiest person in the world.

Today was their ten-month anniversary. Today was also the day she would share her secret with Steven.

She'd never expected on their wedding day that marriage could be this wonderful. Oh, she'd loved Steven. Loved him desperately. She'd known from the very start that she was lucky to have him love her in return. Steven was the most wonderful, kindest, most tender, gentlest man she'd ever known. But she hadn't known marriage could be this good.

Soon it would be even better.

She touched her belly, flat and trim. In a few more months there'd be no disguising the baby that was growing inside her.

Steven's baby.

They would make such a perfect home for this child. He—or she—would be loved and cherished. He would never have to yearn for a father's or mother's approval the way Erika had. He would have a whole family with lots and lots of brothers and sisters. No lonely, only children for this family. Steven and Erika wanted a basketball team, at the very least.

A shudder passed through Erika, a memory, unbidden, intruding on her happiness.

I wish I knew her name.

As quickly as it came, Erika pushed the thought away. She'd learned several tricks for controlling those unwanted memories. She'd had to. Otherwise, every time Dallas came to their apartment with the latest in his long string of girlfriends, she would have gone crazy, the reminders too painful, the shame too deep. So she'd learned the art of denial, pretending "it" had never happened.

Today of all days was not the time to remember. Today was the happiest of days. Today she would tell Steven he was going to be a daddy.

Her life was perfect. Absolutely perfect.

CHAPTER SEVENTEEN

KIRSTEN STARED AT THE CEILING of the
bedroom of her apartment. Her first morning in Boise.
She'd wanted to sleep in, and here she was, awake at the
crack of dawn. What was she going to do now that her
journey cross-country was over? Her belongings wouldn't
arrive until next week, and she wasn't scheduled to report
to work until Monday.

She sat up, thankful for the inflatable mattress Van
had given her. Her funds were running low, and she
couldn't afford another night in a motel. But she wouldn't
have enjoyed sleeping on the floor, either.

So, now what?

She'd called her mother last night to let her know
she'd arrived safely. She'd also called Van. There was no
one else to call.

Except Erika Welby.

She pushed her long, dark hair away from her face, then rose from the bed and padded barefoot to the bathroom. A glance in the mirror caused her to wince.

Her brown eyes always had a just-woke-up look about them, but her reflection belonged to someone who was more than sleepy. Dark smudges formed half-moons beneath her eyes, and there was an unhealthy pallor in her cheeks. Her curly hair—never easy to control under the best of circumstances—looked as if it hadn't seen a brush in a month.

"Great," she muttered. "Just great."

Without a curtain, Kirsten couldn't use the shower, and she hated washing her hair in the tub. It took forever to get the shampoo rinsed out. But with no other option, she turned on the water, pressed the stopper, and waited for the bathtub to fill.

Forty-five minutes later, her skin clean, her hair blown dry, and wearing a mostly wrinkle-free tank top and a pair of shorts, she felt—and looked—much better. She was also ravenous, and no matter how big her credit-card balance, she intended to have a real breakfast. No Twinkies and OJ for her this morning.

She grabbed the city map, her wallet, and car keys and headed out of her apartment. Time to get to know Boise. Her first stop would be the nearest breakfast-serving restaurant, preferably one with biscuits and country gravy on the menu.

⌒

"You're sure you don't want to come with us, Mom? We're only playing nine holes."

Erika glanced from Ethan, standing on the passenger side of his dad's car, to her husband, already behind the wheel. A chill shivered through her. Steven would resent it if she went along—being with her was the last thing he wanted.

"No thanks. You guys go do your thing." She waved bravely. "Have fun and don't go over par."

At least Steven made the effort to wave in return before starting the car and backing out of the drive.

O God, we're falling apart at the seams.

She blinked away unwanted tears, irritated by their appearance. She already felt as if she'd cried enough to fill Lucky Peak Reservoir.

Steven says he's doing the best he can.

She moved off the front steps and strolled along the flower beds, occasionally reaching down to pull weeds.

But it doesn't feel like his best. It feels like he hates me. He doesn't want to touch me. I feel like we're living in a house made of crystal, as if everything could shatter in an instant.

Purple-and-yellow pansies bobbed their heads in the morning breeze, smiling at her.

They're the only things smiling in this place.

Motley bumped against her leg, then pressed his muzzle against her palm.

"Dumb dog," she whispered as she stroked his head.

I'm like Motley, she realized, *begging Steven to look at me, to touch me . . . to love me.*

Her vision blurred a second time, and she bit the inside of her cheek to keep the tears from falling.

"Hi, Mrs. Welby."

Erika turned to see Susie Fulton, the seven-year-old from next door, skipping across the lawn.

"Can I play with Motley?"

"Sure."

Susie leaned forward and patted her thighs. "C'mere, Motley. C'mere, boy."

The dog almost mowed the child down in his eagerness to obey, hopping around as if his legs were made of springs. Susie giggled, delighted by Motley's show of affection.

Erika smiled, but it was bittersweet.

I want to be free and innocent like Susie. I don't want to feel like my world is collapsing. God, how do we make it back? How can the truth set us free if it destroys us first?

"Where's your ball, Motley?" Susie asked in her high-pitched voice. "Find your ball."

The dog understood the word and bounded off to find any one of a half dozen toys that littered the Welby yard. It wasn't long before he returned, a cracked and fading blue rubber ball in his slobbery mouth.

"Good boy." Susie rewarded Motley with a kiss on the top of the head, then several affectionate pats on his shoulder. "Good boy." She took the ball and tossed it toward the fence. "Get it, Motley. Get it."

The command was needless. Motley was already flying after it, tongue flapping out the right side of his mouth.

Will Steven ever forgive me, Lord? Erika knelt on the lawn to pull more weeds. *I need him to forgive me.*

She remembered the moment she'd first been set free from her secret guilt. She remembered kneeling at her bedside, giving her heart to Christ, awash in the love of God, overwhelmed by it, and knowing He forgave her for all the sins of her past. All of them. Including those times with Dallas. Including giving her baby away, then trying to forget her, as if she'd never existed.

Was I so wrong not to tell Steven? What purpose could it have served?

She found no answers in her heart.

"Motley!" Susie's cry, combined with the squeal of sliding tires, brought Erika to her feet. Before Erika's eyes could find the cause for alarm, Susie screamed.

Thud!

Motley lay in the street in front of a pale blue Toyota. The driver, a young woman, was already out of the vehicle, staring, horrified, gripping the car door with her right hand.

Erika bolted forward, wanting to get to the dog before Susie. *Oh please, God, don't let him be dead.*

She knelt in the street, the asphalt of the road digging into her bare knees. "Motley?"

"I'm so sorry. I didn't see him. I'm so sorry. I—"

Motley whimpered. He was alive . . . for now.

"Is there a vet nearby?" the driver asked. "Will you let me take you there?"

Erika slipped her arms beneath the dog. "Yes," she answered without hesitation. "Please."

Motley whimpered again as she lifted him.

"Susie," Erika said, "go tell your mommy what happened. Ask her to call Dr. Murdoch and say we're on our way. Hurry! *Run!*"

The driver opened the rear door of the Toyota. Erika scarcely gave her a glance before sliding into the backseat, cradling the beloved mutt against herself.

Please, God. I couldn't bear to lose Motley. Not now. Not on top of everything else.

Erika must have given the woman directions to the vet's clinic, although she didn't remember doing so. Nor did she remember rushing inside, her pulse racing, her heart filled with dread.

But somehow, she found herself alone in the waiting area with only the driver of the car, a stranger, for company.

"I'm so sorry," the girl said.

Erika looked at the young woman beside her.

She was pretty, with long, kinky-curly black hair, wispy bangs parted by a cowlick in the center of her forehead. Her eyes, filled with concern, were brown with a coppery ring around the corneas. They reminded Erika of—

She released a tiny gasp, knowing but not believing.

With a nod, the young woman whispered, "I'm Kirsten."

❧

Paula rarely paid a visit to the Hurst Technology site, which was only one reason for Dallas's uneasiness as he rose to greet his wife. Things hadn't been smooth on the home front in the two days since he'd told Paula about him and Erika. Oh, his wife pretended to be okay with it. In fact, she'd acted a whole lot better than he'd expected, but Dallas suspected she wasn't as calm about it as she appeared.

"Hi, beautiful." He searched her face for a clue to her mood.

Paula marched up to his desk and fixed him with a direct stare. "Dallas, I've been thinking. We need to see our lawyer."

His mouth went dry. "What for?"

"That girl. The one who claims to be your daughter. What do you know about her?"

"Nothing really, but—"

"Exactly." She placed her knuckles on his desk and leaned toward him. "We know nothing about her. That's why we need to protect ourselves before it's too late. She's probably after our money."

"I don't think she knows who I am. She couldn't—"

"All the more reason to see Scott now. I'm not about to let some moneygrubbing nobody march into town and threaten our way of life. We've worked too hard for what we have to let that happen. It wasn't your fault Erika was stupid enough to get pregnant. We shouldn't have to pay for her mistake. If she'd had any sense, she would have had an abortion. I would've, in her shoes."

For an instant, Dallas wondered if he really knew his wife at all.

This wasn't the way Kirsten had imagined their first meeting, in a room that smelled of frightened animals, medication, and disinfectant.

No, she'd had something more poignant in mind. For several months and across two thousand four hundred and seventy-two miles, she'd imagined all sorts of scenarios for her first meeting with her birth mother, but never had she pictured this one. Nor had she expected to feel a sudden hope that Erika Welby would come to care about her.

Erika said Kirsten's name softly, as if testing it on her tongue.

Kirsten nodded. "Yes."

"I'm Erika."

"I know."

An awkward silence filled the waiting room. A heartbeat later, Erika looked away, turning her gaze toward the examination room where they'd taken the injured dog.

"I'm sorry," Kirsten said for what seemed the hundredth time. "I didn't see him running into the street. I was looking . . . I was looking for your house number and then I saw you in the yard and when I realized—" She stopped, certain she was babbling like an idiot.

"His name is Motley." Erika's voice lowered. "He belongs to Ethan."

Ethan?

As if Kirsten had spoken her question aloud, Erika answered it. "He's my son."

Her son . . .

My brother . . .

Kirsten had wondered, of course. She'd wondered if she had any siblings, but she'd never been able to find that information. Now she knew of at least one. Ethan. Her half brother.

Or is he my full-blooded brother? Is Steven Welby my father?

Kirsten hadn't the courage to ask. Not yet.

The phone rang. The receptionist answered it. Dogs barked somewhere in the bowels of the building. The wall clock noisily ticked off the seconds as the hand swept around its large, white face.

Kirsten pretended to look elsewhere while studying her birth mother's profile.

Do I look like her?

She wasn't sure. For countless years, she'd wished she looked like somebody.

Or do I resemble my father?

Erika Welby had dark blond hair, unlike Kirsten's ebony locks, but it was just as curly, and if she wasn't mistaken, Erika had the same stubborn cowlick that plagued Kirsten.

A cowlick and naturally curly hair. Was that enough to make them mother and daughter?

Erika glanced at Kirsten, tears in her pale blue eyes.

It was Kirsten's turn to look away, afraid.

Afraid that the dog she'd hit with her car wouldn't survive. Afraid Erika Welby wouldn't like her. Afraid Ethan Welby would hate her. Afraid she would never meet her father. Afraid of all the unknown twists and turns of her future.

Afraid.

CHAPTER EIGHTEEN

THE DRIVE HOME from the veterinarian's was even more awkward than the hour the two women had spent in the waiting area. Motley was suffering from shock and some nasty abrasions, Dr. Murdoch had told Erika when he emerged from the examination room, but the dog was expected to make a full recovery.

"Turn right at the next intersection," Erika instructed softly.

Kirsten held the steering wheel with a white-knuckled grip.

Do I ask her in? Erika wondered. *Do I tell her to come back later?*

She could suggest lunch in a week or two. She could say that she understood Kirsten would need time to get settled. She would be doing the girl a favor.

She's your daughter. Your daughter!

Erika felt a catch in her breath, a flutter in her heart.
My daughter.

"There it is," Erika whispered. "On the right."

"Yes. I see it." Kirsten pulled to the curb rather than into the driveway.

This was her baby girl. How could she have considered not meeting her?

Erika drew a shallow breath and asked, "Would you like to come in?"

Kirsten didn't answer immediately. She took a moment to cut the engine, then relaxed her hold on the wheel. Finally, she turned to meet Erika's gaze. "Yes." Her reply was almost inaudible. "Yes, I would like to come in."

"It isn't anything fancy." It sounded like an apology, and Erika regretted that. She loved her home.

In unison, they opened their respective car doors and got out. Erika waited near the curb while Kirsten came around the front of the Toyota. Then they walked side by side up the driveway. The front door wasn't locked. A good thing since Erika had neither her purse nor the key to the house. Erika led the way inside. "The coffee'll be cold by now. I'll brew another pot. Make yourself comfortable." She waved toward the living room off to her left, then headed down the short hallway to the kitchen.

What do I say to her? What will she say to me?

They weren't supposed to have met like this. They might not have met at all, given a different set of circumstances.

She's my daughter. She's a stranger. God, tell me what to do.

Erika moved about the kitchen on autopilot, pouring the cold coffee down the drain, filling the carafe with water, grinding fresh beans.

She looks so much like Dallas. I wasn't ready for that, Lord. Why wasn't I ready for that?

"This must be Ethan."

Erika whirled around. Kirsten stood in the family room, studying the grouping of photos on the wall above the piano.

"Is he your only son?"

"Yes."

Kirsten pointed at another photograph. "And this is your husband? Ethan's father?"

"Yes." Erika moved forward.

Kirsten turned to look at her. "But he isn't *my* father, is he?"

She stopped still, a breathless pause, then the confession. "No."

The question lay unspoken between them: *Who is my father? What's his name?*

The answer lodged in Erika's throat and wouldn't come loose.

"Does he know about me?" Kirsten asked softly. "My father. Did you tell him I was coming? Does he live here?"

"Yes, he lives here. He knows you're coming."

"Does he . . . does he want to meet me?"

Erika felt as if a giant fist were squeezing the life from her heart. "I don't know. He . . . he hasn't told me."

"I see." Kirsten turned back to the wall of photos.

No, you don't see. You can't see. You can't possibly know

what your coming here has done to me, to Steven, to Ethan or Dallas or Paula. You can't know because . . . because I gave you away.

Erika returned to the coffeemaker.

I never smelled your sweet baby's breath. I never kissed the bottoms of your feet after your bath. I never rocked you to sleep or nursed you at my breast.

The pain in her heart was intense. The yearning for what might have been. The ache for all the memories she'd never made. She'd lost all those years, all those magical moments of a child's life—the first steps, the first tooth, the first day of school, a girl's first kiss and her first broken heart, the first day of driver's ed, her graduation. She'd lost all that and more, and she could never get them back. Another woman had those memories, a woman whom Kirsten thought of as Mom.

But Erika could have tomorrow's memories if she made the effort.

&

"Whose car's that?" Ethan asked as Steven turned past the blue Toyota and into the driveway.

"Nobody's I know."

When the car stopped, Ethan opened the passenger door and got out. "I'll put the clubs away."

"Thanks, Son."

Steven glanced toward the front door. He felt a little better than he had when he left. The time on the golf course had helped to clear his head. Maybe he and Erika could—

"Ethan! Ethan!" Little Susie from next door came racing across the yard. "Where's Motley?"

"Backyard. Why?"

"You mean he's not . . . he isn't dead?" Tears ran down her cheeks.

"Dead?" Ethan looked over the roof of the car at his dad.

Steven took charge. "Why would you think Motley might be dead, Susie?"

"The lady in that blue car—" she pointed at the Toyota—"hit him. Mrs. Welby took him to the doctor, but I didn't see her bring him back."

Ethan bolted toward the house, Steven right behind him. "Mom?" the boy shouted as he entered. "Mom?"

"I'm here, Ethan. In the kitchen."

Son and father rushed down the hall.

"Where's Motley?" Ethan demanded as he burst into the room.

"He's at Dr. Murdoch's," his mother answered. "They kept him overnight for observation, but he'll be fine. Dr. Murdoch said it'll just take a bit of time." Her gaze flicked first to Steven, then toward the family room.

Steven and Ethan both turned around.

Steven's first impression of the stranger was that she was attractive. She was young, perhaps in her early twenties. His second impression was that she might not be a stranger after all. He thought he knew her from someplace, although he couldn't think from where.

"Steven. Ethan. This is Kirsten Lundquist."

The oxygen seemed to be sucked right out of the

room as four people stood there, holding their collective breath.

"Maybe we should sit down," Erika said at last.

Kirsten looked at Ethan. "I'm sorry about your dog. I didn't see him run in front of my car."

"Sounds like he'll be okay," Ethan said.

Kirsten nodded.

"Please, everybody," Erika said, the words strained. "Let's sit."

It wasn't until they each found a place—Erika and Steven on opposite ends of the sofa, Ethan in the matching recliner, and Kirsten in the rocker, the chair farthest from the rest of them—that Steven realized why he'd had the impression of knowing the girl. She looked like Dallas: the same brown eyes that sloped at the outer corners, same thick eyebrows and long lashes, same jet-black hair, same olive complexion. But she also resembled Erika with her dimples and her curls.

Kirsten looked like Dallas . . . and like Erika.

Steven ventured a glance at his son. He felt sick in the pit of his stomach, knowing Ethan had seen the resemblances, too. It made Steven angry at Kirsten— and ashamed for his wife.

Kirsten didn't have to be told Steven Welby didn't want her in his home. She could feel it. His resentment pulsed from him like a heartbeat.

She rose. "I think I'd better go."

Erika stood, too, not saying a word. She twisted her hands at her waist like one of those silent-movie heroines. It would have been funny if it weren't so tragic.

It took all of Kirsten's willpower not to run from the house. Instead, she looked at each member of this family and held their gazes long enough to show she wasn't afraid. Then she headed for the front door. She was already down the steps before Erika's voice stopped her.

"I have your number, Kirsten. I'll call you . . . I'll call you soon."

Why call? You don't want me here, either. You don't want me around one bit more than your husband does.

She was dangerously close to tears.

"I'll call you soon," Erika repeated.

I wouldn't care if you never called me if I knew how else to find my father. I don't care anything about you. I already have a mom.

Walking toward her car, Kirsten nodded but she didn't look back, not even for an instant.

CHAPTER NINETEEN

DALLAS AND PAULA met with their lawyer, Scott Monroe, on Friday. During the time they were in his office— at the healthy rate of four hundred dollars per billing hour— Scott reeled off a long list of legal mumbo jumbo and assured them he would find the best way to protect the Hurst assets.

"In the meantime," Scott said at the close of the meeting, "see what you can learn about the girl."

Those words of advice stayed with Dallas the remainder of the day, and by Saturday morning, he knew he couldn't put off making a call.

The phone was answered on the third ring. "Hello?"

"Erika. It's me. Dallas."

A pause, then, "Hello, Dallas."

"Listen, I . . . I need to talk to you. About . . . well, you know."

"About Kirsten."

"Yeah."

"We met her a couple days ago."

"You saw her? She's in Boise already?"

"She came to the house."

His palms were sweating. "She was there, huh?" He moved the receiver to his left ear, then dried his now-free right hand on his pant leg.

"Yes."

"How'd it go?"

She sighed, her breath whispering through the phone line. "Not good."

He wondered what that meant. Was Kirsten rude? hateful? ugly? greedy? What?

"She hit Motley with her car. We had to take him to the vet's."

Dallas muttered a curse.

"It wasn't her fault. It just happened. And Motley's fine. He's home now and lapping up all the pampering he can get."

Dallas didn't care about the dog. What he cared about was Scott's warning, about how Dallas needed to learn more about the girl. "Erika, are you sure she's who she says she is? Are you sure she isn't pulling a fast one?"

"Oh, Dallas. There isn't any doubt."

"You can't be sure from only one meeting. She could be some con artist. Who knows how she got ahold of the adoption information? With the Internet, anything's possible. Maybe we should get a blood test, check the DNA."

"She looks exactly like you."

His throat constricted.

"Even Steven and Ethan noticed the resemblance," Erika added.

A daughter who resembled him.

What was a man supposed to feel when he heard something like that? What was he supposed to think?

What Dallas felt was old. He'd wanted a baby, a son to carry on his name. What he had was a nearly twenty-two-year-old daughter he'd never seen.

"She looks exactly like you."

He took a deep breath. "What did you tell her about me?"

"I told her you knew she was coming, but that's all. She didn't stay long. It was a bit awkward. I . . . I'm going to call her this afternoon."

"Maybe you should let it go, Erika. Maybe she realizes her mistake and will go back to wherever she came from."

There was a lengthy silence on the other end of the line, then, "I don't want her to go back. I want to know her."

"Think of the complications. From the little I've heard from Steven, things aren't good between you and him because of her. Am I right? Her coming here hasn't made things fun at my house, either. We're trying to have a baby of our own, and Paula thinks this girl's after something."

"Dallas," Erika said, her voice soft but firm, "listen to me. It may have been a job that brought Kirsten to Boise, but I believe it's more than that. God's brought her here for a reason."

"Maybe it's the devil's work. Not God's." He said it more out of habit than anything else. After ten years, jabbing at Erika's and Steven's faith was a conditioned response.

She ignored him. "God's sovereign. He's in control, and He loves me, Dallas. As long as I trust Him, whatever happens, it'll work together for my good." There was another silence before she added, "Dallas, Kirsten's my daughter, and I don't want to lose any more time with her."

He noticed she didn't say *our* daughter.

"No matter what the circumstances of her birth, no matter why she came to Boise or what she wants from me, I want to get to know my firstborn child. I want to love her."

"Firstborn child . . ."

The words burrowed into Dallas's chest and stayed there, like a sliver just under the skin—small, irritating, painful.

⁓

Erika didn't move away from the phone after hanging up. She stood there, thinking about the things she'd said. She'd spoken words of faith and trust to Dallas, but now, in the quiet of her kitchen, in a home, a family, that had been fractured, she wondered if she could walk them out. Could she believe God really was in control?

The growling noise of a power tool drew Erika's gaze to the window. Steven was trimming the shrubbery.

Anything to avoid being in the house with me.

She felt the sting of tears again—a too common occurrence these days.

"Hey, Mom!" Ethan called from the hallway.

She wiped her eyes with the backs of her hands, then turned as her son entered the room.

"Can I borrow a few bucks? I need to put some gas in the tank, and I'm running short of cash."

"Sure," she said, reaching for her purse on the counter near the telephone. "I think I've got a ten."

"Mr. Campanella's got my paycheck at the store. I'll pay you back as soon as I can get to the bank."

Erika held out the ten-dollar bill. "Do you work today?"

"Until five." He took the money, then headed for the refrigerator. "Did I tell you he's talking about retiring?"

"Who? Mr. Campanella?"

"Yeah. Guess it's about time. Some days he doesn't remember what he ordered from the suppliers or who he's got scheduled to work."

"What will he do with the store?"

"Sell it, I guess. He doesn't have any family." Ethan took a plastic milk carton from the refrigerator door. He unscrewed the lid, then placed it to his lips and drained it dry.

It was such a wonderfully normal thing for a teenage boy to do, it somehow kept Erika's precariously tipping world from being completely upended. She wanted to hug him.

He saw her watching and gave her an apologetic grin. "Sorry."

"It's okay."

"No." His grin vanished. "I mean, I'm sorry for more than drinking out of the carton. I'm sorry for how I acted last week. After you told me about Kirsten."

"It's okay," she repeated, her throat tight.

"It isn't okay, Mom." He walked across the kitchen to her.

How like his father he looked.

"I talked to Cammi about what's going on. I told her about Kirsten. I hope it's all right with you. I needed to tell somebody."

Erika nodded.

"She was asking all sorts of questions about Kirsten, and I didn't know any of the answers. It got me thinking that it must've been hard for you when she was born. I mean, you were just my age when you had her."

Again, Erika nodded.

Her son looked beyond her shoulder toward the window. "I have to admit, I see how it could happen. I know kids who . . . well, you know, do things they shouldn't. Like drinking and messing around and stuff. Even some of my Christian friends."

She reached out to touch his arm. The gesture brought his gaze back to her.

"Not me and Cammi, Mom, if that's what you're wondering." Ethan took a step back. "I gotta get going or I'll be late to work. I just wanted you to know that I'm cool with whatever you decide about Kirsten. You know, about us getting to know her and stuff."

"Thank you, Ethan," Erika said softly. "That means more than you know."

He grinned again, then left the kitchen.

Erika walked to the patio door and looked outside, where Steven still wielded the power trimmer.

Ethan's cool with it. She wished she could shout the words at Steven. *Ethan's cool with it. Why can't you be?*

JUNE 1985

In the wee hours of the night, Erika sat in the rocking chair Grams had given her, nursing two-week-old Ethan, her cheeks damp with tears.

There would be no Welby basketball team for Steven to coach. There would be no more babies for him to raise.

"You're lucky to be alive," many had told her while she was still in the hospital.

She didn't feel lucky. She felt heartbroken, inconsolable.

And she couldn't help wondering, in the darkest corner of her heart, if this had happened because of what she'd done five years before in Boston. Was this—the inability to bear more children—her punishment for not wanting her firstborn?

"I love you," she whispered to Ethan. "You're the most wanted baby in all the world. I promise to be a good mother, to be there for you whenever you need me."

"Me, too," came Steven's voice, gravelly with sleep, from behind her.

She looked at him through a misty gaze as he knelt beside the rocker. He kissed the baby's downy soft head, then looked up at Erika, lifting a hand to her cheek, cupping it gently.

"I love you," he said. "You look so beautiful like this, holding our son."

Her throat constricted. "But there won't be—"

"Shh." He placed a finger against her lips, silencing her. "Nothing's going to change the way I feel about you, sweetheart. Nothing. I'm going to love you forever. And we're a family, you and me and Ethan. What more could anybody ask for?"

CHAPTER TWENTY

KIRSTEN PAUSED INSIDE the entrance to the hardware store and looked around, trying to get her bearings.

It wasn't a large store, but there seemed to be plenty here. The aisles were narrow, the shelves tall and cluttered. She hadn't a clue how to find the things she needed.

The truth was, she was tired and out of sorts, and the work of moving in had only begun.

At the back of the store, she saw a clerk in a red vest standing on a ladder, reaching for a box on the top shelf. An elderly woman stood nearby, watching him.

"Not that one, young man," the customer said loudly. "The black one."

The clerk moved his fingers to the next box to the right and glanced down.

"Yes. That's the one."

The clerk slid the box forward until he could grasp it with both hands; then he pulled it the rest of the way off the shelf and stepped down.

"Thank you so much," the woman said, holding out her arms for the box. "You've been most helpful."

"Let me carry it up front for you, ma'am." He turned toward the front of the store.

It was Ethan Welby. Kirsten almost turned to leave, but then he saw her. His eyes widened slightly, and she knew she'd been recognized, too.

He said, "I'll be right with you."

Kirsten nodded, then moved down the nearest aisle, pretending to look for something—although at the moment she couldn't remember what she needed—while Ethan rang up the elderly woman's purchase.

My brother.

She'd thought of him often in the past two days, wondering what sort of young man he was, wondering what he thought about her.

"Hi," Ethan said as he approached her a few minutes later. "Sorry to keep you waiting."

She turned toward him. "That's all right."

"I'm all alone here right now. The owner, Mr. Campanella, had to run an errand."

She realized he was as uncertain about what to say as she was. She gave him a slight smile. "How's your dog?"

"Mom picked him up from the vet's. He's doin' okay."

"I'm glad." She shifted her weight from one foot to the other. "I was so scared after I hit him. He came out of nowhere." Kirsten moistened her lips with her tongue.

"Can I help you find something?" Ethan asked.

"Please." She nodded again. "I need a few basic tools. Screwdrivers. Hammer. Nails. Picture hangers. That sort of stuff."

"Getting moved in, huh?" He motioned for her to follow him down the aisle.

"My furniture and boxes arrived this morning. I wasn't expecting the van until next week, so it's a good thing I was at the apartment." She was babbling, but she couldn't seem to stop herself. "The movers pretty much dumped everything inside the door and left, so now I'm trying to put things together, make sure the furniture's where I want it, hang a few pictures."

Ethan stopped and looked at her. "Are you doing it all alone?"

She shrugged. "I'm the only one there is."

He glanced away, then back again. "I could help. I'm off in half an hour. Soon as my boss gets back."

Kirsten wasn't sure how to answer. She suspected that his offer was made partly out of curiosity, partly because he was trying to do the right thing.

"Mom would want me to help you," he added.

She should refuse. She didn't want to be an obligation. Still, it would be a chance to learn more about Ethan and Erika, which might, in turn, lead to learning something about her father.

"I suppose it would go faster with two," she answered at last.

"Great. We'll get the stuff you need, then I can follow you back to your place in my car."

ॐ

Erika found Steven in the garage, where he was attempting to repair the mower engine.

It seemed she was continually searching for him. He never stayed in the same room with her any longer than he absolutely had to. The most time he spent with her was at night, while he slept, lying as far away as he could get without falling off the bed.

"Steven?" she said, trying to keep the nervousness from her voice. "I want to invite Kirsten to come to dinner after church tomorrow. Is that all right with you?"

Her husband didn't look up. "Do whatever you want, Erika. You will anyway."

That wasn't fair. She'd always cared what Steven thought, had heeded his advice. Why was he acting like this? Why did he have to say such hurtful things?

She clenched her hands. "Will you at least try to make her feel welcome?"

She could see the tension in his jaw, knew he was fighting for control over his anger, an anger that was ever present these days.

"I'd rather she didn't come, but I'll try not to be rude to her if she does."

Erika supposed that was something.

"Do you have any idea how hard this is for me?" he asked.

"I think I do."

"I doubt it." He looked at her, eyes accusing. "Do you ever wish you were with him instead?"

"With *Dallas?* Oh, Steven. No. Not ever."

His expression said he didn't believe her.

"Steven, I—"

"Plan your dinner, Erika." He looked down at the mower, picked up a wrench with his right hand—a hand smeared with black grease—and placed it over a bolt, then gave the wrench a firm twist.

Somehow, Erika felt that twist in her heart.

Steven winced at the sound of the closing door.

Lord?

Silence.

There was a lot of silence in his life these days. Between him and his wife. Between him and his God. Silence that Steven had put there.

How do I get past these feelings?

The resentment ate at him, tearing up his insides. Oh, he tried to say and do the right things. Hadn't he asked Dallas to forgive him? Yes. Had he refused to have Kirsten in his home? No.

But that was all on the outside.

Inside, in his heart, the enmity festered. Inside his resentful heart he still wanted things to be as they were before.

Kirsten glanced in her rearview mirror. The red-and-white Chevy was right behind her, Ethan at the wheel.

"This is crazy," she muttered as she switched on her signal, then turned right into the apartment complex's parking lot. "I shouldn't have agreed to it." It seemed lately she was doing a lot of things she shouldn't.

She wound her way past carports and over speed bumps toward the back of the complex. Her apartment was in Building G, farthest from the clubhouse, pool, and tennis courts.

She pulled the Toyota into her covered parking spot, cut the engine, then grabbed her sack from the hardware store and got out. Ethan waited for her on the sidewalk.

He was a tall kid. Height was something Kirsten always noticed about people because at five-ten she was tall for a girl. He looked a lot more like his dad than his mom. Same dark brown hair as Steven Welby, same blue eyes.

She wondered if, when she and Ethan stood side by side, anyone would guess they were brother and sister.

"Ready?" Ethan asked.

"Yes," she answered. "I'm ready. Come see what you got yourself into."

It turned out that bringing Ethan Welby to her place wasn't a mistake. He worked hard, followed orders, and knew how to do some things she wouldn't have figured out for days, if ever. Within a relatively short period of time, Kirsten's apartment went from being a total disaster to, if not perfect, very livable.

In celebration, she ordered a large combo pizza delivered, along with two salads with Thousand Island dressing and a liter of root beer—all of them her favorites and, as it turned out, his, too.

Kirsten brought utensils, paper plates, and glasses from the kitchen and set them on the marred coffee table she'd bought the previous year at a yard sale for fifteen dollars. When the food arrived, she set it there, too. Then she and Ethan sat on the floor across from each other.

"Dig in," she said, flipping open the pizza-box lid.

Ethan nodded, then closed his eyes for only a few moments.

Was he praying? It appeared so.

Weird. She couldn't remember the last time she'd been with somebody who said grace over their food. It sure wasn't anything they'd done in the Lundquist home. She'd often heard her mother say, "Why should I thank God? I got everything we have through the sweat of my own brow."

Even as a child, Kirsten had understood the bitterness revealed in that remark.

Ethan helped himself to a large piece of pizza, then smiled at Kirsten. "I'm starved. Thanks for doing this."

"It's the least I could do after all the help you were."

He shrugged off her words. "Hey, what's family for?"

Family. Her heart fluttered. *We're family.*

"Does it feel strange to you, too?" Ethan leaned forward. "I mean, having a brother you never met until now."

She set down the slice of pizza, her throat too tight to swallow. "Yes, it's strange."

"I always wanted a brother or a sister, but Mom couldn't have any more kids after me."

"She couldn't?"

"No. She almost died when I was born. They had to do a hysterectomy."

"I didn't know."

If Ethan found her reply fatuous he gave no indication. "Mom's real glad you found her."

Another unexpected skip of the heart. "Really?"

"Yeah. Really."

"But your dad isn't."

A thoughtful frown furrowed Ethan's brow. "Dad never knew Mom had a baby before me. It sorta rocked him, finding out about you now. But he'll come around eventually."

Kirsten wasn't so sure.

"It was a real shocker," Ethan added, "seeing how much you look like your dad."

Time screeched to a halt. Kirsten stared at Ethan, her mouth parted, her throat dry, her heart pounding.

Ethan's eyes widened as if he suddenly realized what he'd said.

"You know who my father is?"

He hesitated a moment before nodding.

"Who?"

It was obvious Ethan was wrestling with what to say, so Kirsten pressed him, giving no quarter. "Who's my father, Ethan? What's his name? You have to tell me. I've got a right to know. You must see that."

After what seemed a long while, he answered, "His name's Dallas." He spoke the name with great reluctance.

"Dallas what?"

"Dallas Hurst."

"Hurst," she whispered. "Dallas Hurst. And you say I look like him?"

"Yeah. A lot."

I look like my father.

CHAPTER TWENTY-ONE

KIRSTEN STOOD ON THE SMALL DECK outside her apartment's living room, her back against the doorjamb, the portable phone in her right hand.

"It's very pretty here," she told her mother. "The city's right up against the mountains, and the river is so clear you can see the rocky bottom in most places. You should come for a visit soon."

"I'd love to, but there's no way I could afford it. Not right now, anyway."

Kirsten felt a wave of homesickness wash over her. "Well, we could both sock a little money away here and there. Sometimes you can find great fare bargains on the Internet."

"I don't know if I'd trust buying a ticket that way.

What if someone stole my credit-card number? I've seen those stories on *60 Minutes* and *Dateline*."

Kirsten shook her head. Her mom had no understanding of computers or the Internet. There was no point in trying to explain how it worked.

"Have you met her yet?" Donna asked after a moment of silence.

Kirsten didn't need to ask whom she meant. "Yes. I'm going to her house for dinner today."

"What's she like?"

"She seems nice, Mom. She's got a son. His name's Ethan, and he just turned seventeen. He's nice, too."

"Nice." There was a wealth of insecurity voiced in that one, small word.

"Oh, Mom. I love you so much." Tears welled in Kirsten's eyes. "No matter what happens here with Erika and her family, my feelings for you aren't going to change. But you need to let me do this without guilt. Please."

"I'm sorry, Kirsten. I didn't mean to make you feel guilty about anything. I guess I'm afraid I'll lose you to her. I didn't think I would be, but I am."

"You're not going to lose me."

She heard her mother sniffling.

"I miss you, Mom."

"I miss you, too." Donna sighed deeply, then said, "It's time for me to dash."

Kirsten understood. Her mother didn't want her to know she was about to cry.

"Call me again soon, Kirsten. Okay?"

"Okay. I will. I love you."

"I love you, too."

"Bye, Mom."

The line went dead.

༈

Erika checked the table setting for the umpteenth time. She moved the silk flower centerpiece a smidgen to the left, then a fraction toward the windows. She wondered if she should get out her good dishes rather than the everyday ones. No, that would seem too formal. She wanted Kirsten to feel comfortable.

The doorbell rang.

"She's here," Erika whispered.

"I'll get it," Ethan called from the hall.

Moments later, she heard him open the door, speak a greeting, invite Kirsten inside. She waited, still breathless, for the two of them to appear.

"Here she is," Ethan announced as he led the way into the dining room.

Erika stepped forward. "Hello, Kirsten." Should she shake her hand or hug her? She did neither. "We're so glad you came."

Kirsten nodded, the tiniest of smiles curving the corners of her mouth. "Thanks."

"I hope you're hungry," Ethan said. "Mom's Swedish meatballs are the best."

Kirsten looked at Erika again. "Maybe you'll share the recipe. I'm not much of a cook, though."

"I'd be happy to share."

Erika thought they sounded like bad actors reading a bad script.

"Before we eat," Ethan said, "is it okay if I take Kirsten out to see Motley?"

"Oh, I'd like that," Kirsten replied. "I've felt so bad about him. I'd love to see how he's doing. If . . . if it's all right, that is."

Erika nodded, then watched the two young people—her son and her daughter—walk from the room.

My children. My children together.

~

Ethan and Kirsten knelt on the lawn on either side of Motley. The dog rolled onto his back, relishing the double dose of attention.

Ethan stroked Motley's exposed belly and said, "What a ham. I think he's doing this for your benefit."

"I'm glad he's okay." She brushed the hair away from the dog's eyes, then leaned forward and kissed his nose. "I promise to be more careful in the future, fella."

They were both silent for a while before Ethan asked, "Are you nervous? About being here, I mean."

"A little," she lied, meeting his gaze. *A lot!* she told him with her eyes.

"So . . ." Ethan sat back on his heels and rested his palms on his thighs. "Now that you've had a chance to look me over a couple of times, how do you *really* feel about having a brother?"

The truth was, Kirsten liked this boy more and more, especially now, when she knew he was trying to calm her nerves.

She mimicked his position, then cocked her head to one side and pretended to study him. "You're okay," she said at last. "And better looking than your dog."

Ethan laughed. Motley hopped up, tail wagging hard, striking the humans on either side. Saliva dripped from the dog's tongue as he shoved his muzzle close to his master's nose.

"You've been insulted, boy," Ethan said as he ruffled the dog's ears.

Kirsten hoped this good-natured banter boded well for the rest of the day.

⌇

Steven stood at the bedroom window, watching. He saw Ethan gently push Motley away, trying to get the dog to lie down. Ethan said something, and Kirsten smiled.

Her smile . . .

Steven would never get used to that smile. It was broad and bright, like a thousand-watt lightbulb. At first, her lips quivered. Then her mouth parted, revealing straight, white teeth. At the same time, her brown eyes widened and her brows lifted in a look of amused surprise.

It was identical to the way Dallas Hurst smiled.

Steven's gut twisted.

She has no right to be here. She doesn't belong. She isn't part of this family. I don't want her to be a part of it.

Steven heard the patio door slide open, then Erika calling, "Come and get it, you two."

You two . . .

Steven tapped his fist against the wall, wanting to hit it—the same way he'd hit Dallas.

CHAPTER TWENTY-TWO

STEVEN'S ANIMOSITY TOWARD KIRSTEN was like an uninvited guest at their table. Erika felt his resentment and was certain Kirsten could feel it, too.

Seated across the table from Kirsten, Steven remained stubbornly mute as he ate, his gaze locked on his plate.

Why can't you forgive me, Steven? Don't you understand that I wish she were your daughter instead of Dallas's? I wish she had blue eyes instead of brown and brown hair instead of black. I wish we could have raised her with Ethan and watched them play together as a brother and sister should. I wish I had an album full of her baby pictures, right beside our son's. I wish I could have seen her take her first steps and heard her speak her first word and worried about her when she went off to school for the first time. Oh, how I wish all of those things. But I can't change the past. I can't. Not even for you.

187

He glanced up, as if knowing she wanted to say something to him.

You can help me decide the future, if only you will. Please, Steven. Please.

He looked down again, his face like stone.

"Did you go to college?" Ethan asked Kirsten. Almost single-handedly he had kept the conversation going, never allowing the small gathering to fall into awkward silences. Mostly they'd talked about Kirsten's drive across the country, her impressions of Boise, her new job.

"Business school," Kirsten answered him. "My mom couldn't afford college tuition, and I was only an average student, so scholarships weren't available."

Erika wondered if things would have been different—better—for Kirsten if Erika had kept her, raised her. Would Kirsten have been an above-average student? Might she have gone to college?

Oh, the guilt, the unending, unanswerable questions.

Ethan leaned his forearms on the table. "Tell us about your family."

Her son was fearless, Erika thought, knowing she wouldn't have asked. Not yet, at any rate, even though she'd longed to know.

"My adoptive father's name was Felix. He died when I was two."

"That's rough," Ethan said. "Must've been hard growing up without a dad."

Kirsten's gaze moved from him to Erika, then to the centerpiece on the table. "Yes, in lots of ways it was very hard."

188

Erika suspected there was more beneath those words than what appeared on the surface. More guilt came on the heels of that suspicion. Guilt and a renewed wish to have known Kirsten as she was growing up, regret for all she would never know about her daughter.

"Both sets of my grandparents died before I came along, so I never knew—"

"Hey," Ethan interrupted. "That's not true anymore. You've got grandparents. Wait until you meet Grams. Louisa Scott's her real name. Anyway, she's our great-grandmother. You're gonna love her. And Grandpa James, too. Mom's dad. He's a little harder to get to know. He's kind of testy, but his bark's worse than his bite. Huh, Mom?"

Erika managed a weak smile and a nod even as she felt the blood draining from her head.

Ethan said something else, but Erika no longer listened. Instead she imagined her son taking his half sister to meet their grandfather. She pictured the look on her dad's face when he discovered he had an illegitimate granddaughter. She saw the condemnation in his eyes and felt the scorching shame his words would hail down upon her.

I can't put it off any longer. I'm going to have to tell him.

༈

At the end of the meal, Steven said, "Ethan and I'll take care of the dishes."

Kirsten saw the flicker of something in her birth

mother's eyes but wasn't sure what it was. Gratitude, perhaps. Maybe a bit of surprise. For that matter, Kirsten was surprised herself. Steven Welby hadn't said that much throughout dinner and had seemed pretty sullen.

Erika turned toward Kirsten. "Let's go to the living room."

Kirsten nodded, then followed Erika.

Two things Kirsten had noticed during her two visits to this house: The Welby home had a warm, lived-in feel about it, and unlike Donna Lundquist, Erika apparently had no taste for kitsch.

Kirsten felt an obligatory twinge of shame, as if by her thoughts she'd betrayed her mother. Still, it was true. Donna didn't have a natural talent for decorating. Erika did.

The living room was feminine, even delicate, in appearance. The overstuffed, skirted sofa was upholstered in a floral pattern of peach, lavender, and cream. The accompanying chair was covered in a solid peach fabric. End tables of light oak, on either side of the couch, held lamps with cream-colored shades. In the center of the coffee table were two candles and a large Bible; on both ends, in the nooks underneath the table, were what appeared to be artsy, coffee-table-type books: *Norman Rockwell, A Sixty Year Retrospective; The Art of God; Mary, Did You Know?* A large, gilt-framed mirror on the wall opposite the window made the room seem bigger than it was.

As if reading Kirsten's thoughts, Erika said, "This is really my room. The guys don't feel comfortable with the flowers or the colors. Too feminine, they say."

"I like it."

Erika smiled and motioned to the sofa.

Kirsten took a seat.

Erika sat beside her, her smile fading as she met Kirsten's gaze. "I know you must have a hundred questions."

An understatement.

"No matter what they are, I'll try to answer them the best I can."

Kirsten had both longed for and dreaded this moment. Now it was here, and she didn't know where to start, what to ask first.

"Would you like to see some photographs?" Erika offered.

Kirsten released a relieved breath. "Please."

Erika opened the door on one of the end tables and withdrew a thick photo album, about the size of an unabridged dictionary. She placed it on the coffee table but didn't open it. "Ethan told you the name of your . . . your birth father, didn't he?"

Kirsten's pulse quickened again. "Yes."

"What else did he tell you?"

"Only that I look like him."

"You *do* look like him. Your eyes especially." Erika lifted a hand, as if to touch Kirsten, then lowered it again. "There were only two people who knew about you until we got your letter. My grandmother and me. Nobody else knew. Not Steven. Not Dallas. Nobody."

Kirsten noticed a sheen of tears glistening Erika's eyes, and she had to swallow hard to rid herself of a lump in her throat.

"I fell in love with Steven when I was fifteen, but when he left for college . . . Dallas and I—Dallas was Steven's best friend. Both he and I missed Steven. We didn't mean to—" She drew in a ragged breath. "It just happened."

It just happened.

Funny, the way those three words seemed to say so much more than they should have. They hurt. Hurt worse than Kirsten wanted them to.

It just happened.

Erika continued with her story, not pausing again until she reached the time of Ethan's birth, nearly five years after Kirsten. "I want you to know something," Erika added at the end. "You were never forgotten. I kept you a secret because it seemed the best thing to do, for everyone concerned. But you were never forgotten. Not in my mind and not in my heart."

"I wasn't?" Kirsten whispered, not meaning to speak the words aloud.

"No, you weren't." Erika swiped at tears on her cheeks. "Sometimes when I sat rocking Ethan, when he was a baby, in the middle of the night, I'd pretend I knew what it was like to hold you, too. I'd see little girls on the street, with their hair all brushed and shiny and fastened with ribbons, and I'd wish I could have dressed you up that way." She pulled the photo album onto her lap, staring at its cover. "And every August first, I've awakened at five in the morning, the hour you were born, to wish you happy birthday and pray that you were loved and healthy." Lifting her gaze toward Kirsten once again, she said, "I'm thankful to God that you had the courage to look for me."

Something gave way inside Kirsten as she listened. Maybe it was unforgiveness for the times in her childhood when she'd felt unloved, unwanted, discarded. Maybe it was her resistance to care for this woman more than she thought she should. Whatever it was, Kirsten felt lighter of heart than she had in a long, long while.

Erika felt both exhilarated and exhausted by the time her daughter left the house. She could scarcely believe the time when she entered the kitchen and looked at the clock on the wall. It was after six o'clock. Where had the hours gone?

Ethan had poked his head into the living room sometime during her visit with Kirsten and announced he was going to Cammi's and would be back before nine. The house was so quiet now, Erika wondered if Steven had left, too.

But he hadn't.

When Erika walked into the bedroom a short while later, she found him lying on his back on the bed, one arm draped over his eyes. The curtains had been drawn, casting the room in shadows. Thinking he was asleep, she started to leave the room.

"Is she gone?"

Erika stopped and turned back. "Yes."

He sat up, then raked his hair with his fingers.

"Thanks for doing the dishes," she said.

He grunted.

"We had a good talk." She stepped deeper into the room. "It would have been all right if you'd joined us."

He looked toward her. "I'm not interested. Okay?"

Anger overtook her. "Grow up, Steven."

"What?"

"I said, grow up. I thought we were a team. I thought we were supposed to help each other in times of trial and testing."

"I'm not the one who—"

"Oh yes. That's right. I forgot. You led a perfect life while you were away at college. You wrote to me faithfully, and you never dated any other girls, and you were as pure as the driven snow when we got married." The words tumbled out of her. "Well, excuse me for thinking the last eighteen years of marriage counted for something." She stormed out of the bedroom.

Steven followed her. "You could have told me. You could have said something years ago."

"Exactly when should I have done it?" She whirled about in the hallway. "When you called me for that first date after you got back from college? When you asked me to marry you? When I got pregnant with Ethan?" She waved at him. "You couldn't have handled it. You can't even handle it now when you're supposed to be more mature."

"You *lied* to me."

"Yes, I lied. And I said I'm sorry. I've asked you to forgive me. But you can't, can you? You can't bring yourself to forgive me."

"I'm doing the best I can."

Erika turned and headed for the kitchen again. "Then you need to try harder."

"What did you say?" Steven demanded, hard on her heels.

She turned again, shouting, "I said I need a husband who'll support me. I said I need you to *act* like you believe what you say you believe. That you're *part* of this marriage. Do you think you're the only one struggling here? You're not. Why don't you try thinking of someone other than yourself for a change? What about me and Ethan? Stop being such a self-righteous jerk."

As soon as the words were out of her mouth, she wished them back. But they hung there in the silence between them, like a cat about to pounce on a mouse.

Steven was the first to walk away, retreating to his workshop in the garage, leaving Erika alone again.

So alone.

CHAPTER TWENTY-THREE

ERIKA CHOSE A TABLE in the corner at the back of Moxie Java. The coffee shop was mostly empty in this awkward time between the rush of early-morning commuters and late-morning shoppers.

Her friend Barb held Erika's hand as she poured out her story, holding nothing back now, confessing it all, from the very beginning right up through her horrid fight with Steven the night before.

"I'm going over to tell my dad when I leave here," Erika said when her tale was done. "I can't put it off any longer."

Barb nodded, then said, "I take it Steven hasn't sought counsel."

"No. Not that he's told me." She sighed. "But then, he doesn't talk to me these days."

"I think you should see one of the pastors. Tell them what's going on, and see if they won't approach Steven." She shook her head. "No marriage works well as an armed camp."

"I shouldn't have said what I did to him." Erika dropped her gaze. "But I was so angry and tired of feeling to blame for everything. I'm tired of being judged and found wanting."

"Of course you're tired. You've been on an emotional roller coaster. It's understandable that something like this is full of both pain and joy."

"Yes." How good it was to have someone understand.

"You aren't to blame for everything, Erika. You need to remember that. Each of us is responsible for our own actions, not the actions of others. Don't take that burden on."

Erika swallowed the lump in her throat. "Easier said than done."

A synthesized bing announced the arrival of new customers. Erika's gaze was drawn toward the door. And there was Paula Hurst, hanging on the arm of Warren Carmichael, the CEO of a major Northwestern grocery chain. Erika knew his name because she'd seen him in countless television ads during the past year.

Paula's throaty laughter carried across the coffee shop to the corner where Erika sat. Erika felt a breathless moment of surprise, followed by a sudden certainty of what was before her. There was no mistaking the intimate nature of Paula's touch or the expression on her face. These weren't business associates meeting over coffee.

Erika sucked in a tiny breath, not sure what to do, wanting to look away, yet unable to make herself do so.

As if hearing the sound, Paula glanced in her direction.

Oh, the absolute finesse, the stunning self-assurance in the way Paula disengaged herself from her lover and made her way between the tables toward Erika and Barb.

"Hello, Erika."

"Paula."

"I didn't expect to see you this morning."

No, I don't suppose you did.

"Are you planning to come to our Fourth of July bash? We didn't get your RSVP."

"I don't know yet."

Paula's smile was artificially sweet. "Why, it wouldn't be the same without you and Steven. You know that. You've simply got to come."

Everybody who was anybody in Idaho—corporation presidents and chief financial officers, mayors from towns throughout the Treasure Valley, state senators and representatives, the governor and his wife— attended Mr. and Mrs. Dallas Hurst's annual Fourth of July celebration. It was *the* event of the summer. Erika had always felt out of place among all the dignitaries and powermongers, but she'd gone because the Hursts were their friends.

"I'll check with Steven and let you know," she said.

Paula glanced over her shoulder. "Well, I'd better get back to business. Mr. Carmichael and I are finalizing the details for a multimillion-dollar complex." She looked at Erika again. "No rest for the wicked, as my grand-mother used to say."

Erika watched the younger woman walk away, then lowered her eyes, whispering, "Not this, too."

~

Steven had accomplished absolutely nothing that morn-ing. All he could think about was his fight with Erika. It kept replaying and replaying in his mind, like a horror movie on late-night TV.

Why was it that he could so clearly see the mistakes of his actions, his words, even his feelings, and yet do nothing about them?

He left his office, too restless to sit still another moment. He was already out the front door of the school before he saw Dallas, leaning against his Lexus that was parked at the curb. Steven hadn't seen his friend since the day he'd gone to Hurst Technology to apologize. He'd hoped time and space would change the way he felt. It hadn't.

Dallas straightened. "Got a minute?"

Steven stopped but didn't answer.

"I told Paula I want to meet Kirsten."

Steven clenched his teeth.

"The idea went over like a lead balloon," Dallas went on.

Steven wanted to hit him again. He'd like to smash a fist right into his friend's pearly whites.

Only maybe they weren't friends. Maybe they

hadn't been for a long, long time. Or ever. Would a friend do what Dallas had done? Not in Steven's book.

"Have you met her?" Dallas asked.

"Yes."

"When?"

"She came to dinner yesterday."

"How did it go?"

It was better not to answer, Steven thought. It was better not to admit how much he'd hated having the girl in his home, at his table, how much he'd hated seeing Ethan's easy way with Kirsten, how much he'd hated seeing Erika's hopeful expression, how much he'd hated knowing that she loved her daughter, a daughter who wasn't his.

"I wanted kids," Dallas said. "I've wanted kids of my own for a long time. I just never expected it to happen like this." He muttered a curse. "She's only eight years younger than Paula. Did you know that?"

Sure, he knew. How could he not know, when he'd thought of little other than Kirsten for days on end?

Steven's stomach churned. He rubbed his sweaty palms against his slacks and tried to think of something to say to the man who'd slept with his wife.

He winced inwardly, as he always did at the thought. *Years ago. It happened years ago. You're supposed to forgive them.*

Forgiveness was a decision, not a feeling. He'd come to believe that as he'd studied the Bible. He'd believed it for years. He'd even taught it when he led an adult Sunday school class a few years back.

So why couldn't he make that decision now?

"Look," Steven said gruffly, "I've got to get some-place, and I'm running late. We'll have to talk about this some other time."

"Sure." Dallas's eyes said he knew it was a lie. Steven had no intention of talking about it later.

Steven walked away with long, hurried strides.

૱

Feeling like a condemned prisoner on her way to the gallows, Erika stood on the sidewalk leading up to the front door of her father's house. *God, give me courage.*

She'd told her best friend. She planned to tell her pastor. Now it was time to tell her father.

Drawing a shaky breath, she moved up the walk and rang the bell, then waited. Except in a dire emergency, she wouldn't consider using her key to this lock. Her father had only agreed to give it to her after he fell two years ago and she'd come to look after him while he was laid up with a bum leg.

The door opened, and her father frowned out at her.

"Erika." Trevor James glanced toward the street, then back at his daughter. "What're you doing here this time of day?"

Butterflies bounced off the lining of her stomach. "Morning, Dad."

He grunted—a welcome of sorts—opened the door wider, turned, and walked away, leaving Erika to follow after him.

The ground floor of her girlhood home was not more than nine hundred square feet in size. It had a small living room, a breakfast nook off the tiny kitchen, two bedrooms, and a bath. The laundry was in the unfinished basement, along with the furnace and the curtained-off corner that Grams had called her room when she'd lived there.

Erika noticed the threadbare spots in the gray wool carpet in the living room. She had been in junior high when it was installed. The wallpaper throughout the house was in worse shape, yellowed and curling in all the corners. Erika had pleaded with her father to allow her to strip the walls and paint them. He'd vetoed the idea on more than one occasion. He'd never given her a reason why, but it wasn't because he couldn't afford to make some improvements.

Her dad sat in his La-Z-Boy recliner and picked up that morning's edition of the *Idaho Statesman*, snapping open the local section and beginning to read.

The gesture stung—as his rejections always did.

Erika sat on the sofa. "I came to talk to you."

He glanced over the top of the page.

"It's important, Dad."

He refolded the newspaper and gave her a long-suffering look.

Why does he have to be so impossible? Would it be too much to ask that he love his own daughter?

"Well?" he prompted.

"I have something difficult to say. Something from a long time ago, but it's going to affect all of us a lot from now on." She licked her lips, her mouth and throat bone dry. She considered going to the kitchen for a glass of water.

"Spit it out, girl. I haven't got all day."

ƑEBRUARY 1973

"Turn around," Mommy said, "and let me have a look at you."

Erika was happy to pirouette for her mother, especially in her new taffeta dress.

"You look so pretty, honey. We'd better go show Daddy."

Erika's smile slipped a little. She'd heard her parents arguing last night about her birthday party. Daddy hadn't been happy about the money Mommy spent. It seemed like they argued about a lot of things.

Mommy put an arm around Erika's shoulders and gave her a squeeze. "Don't think badly of your daddy, Erika. He doesn't mean to sound so gruff."

"Then why does he?"

Mommy knelt on the floor. "It's hard to understand adult things when you're just turning ten, but maybe you can understand a little. Daddy's worried about his job. There hasn't been a lot of work for him lately, and he isn't making as much money as he used to. He's afraid he won't be able to provide for us."

"Can't he write another check?"

"If only it were that easy," Mommy answered softly.

It seemed easy enough to Erika. If that's what would make Daddy smile once in a while, she thought he ought to do it. Her best friend's daddy didn't growl at his family the way Erika's did. Anna's daddy teased Anna and her brother, and he kissed their mommy, and he smiled a lot. He even played dolls with Anna when she asked him to.

The thought of asking her daddy to play with her made Erika's stomach feel funny.

Mommy gave her a hug. "We need to just love Daddy a lot. Okay?"

"Maybe he'd be happier if he went with Grams and us to church sometimes. Everybody smiles there."

"Yes, they do, don't they?" But Mommy's own smile looked kind of sad to Erika. "I wish your daddy believed." She kissed her daughter's cheek. "It's important to know Jesus, Erika. There's nothing more important than—"

The doorbell rang, interrupting her mother's words, and Erika squealed with excitement. Her birthday guests were arriving. There would be games and presents and cake and ice cream, and that was what seemed most important to Erika right now.

Even her daddy's scowls couldn't spoil things for her today.

Chapter Twenty-Four

ON HER LUNCH HOUR the first day on her new job, Kirsten went for a walk on the Greenbelt, a pathway that followed the Boise River for miles, right through the heart of the city. Ancient trees—cottonwoods, box elders, birch—with gnarled trunks and leafy branches shaded the cyclists, skateboarders, and joggers from the hot July sun, the air cooled by a gentle breeze off the river's surface.

Kirsten's pace was more leisurely than most. She wanted to take in all the sights and sounds. Already, she'd seen two raccoons, countless squirrels, an industrious beaver, and what she thought was a fox, although she supposed it could have been a small dog. She had been told if she kept a sharp lookout, she might even see an occasional bald eagle, bear, or bobcat.

Now those were things she'd never stumbled upon
in Philadelphia.

Her wireless phone played the *William Tell* Overture,
drawing the gazes of others on the path. Kirsten answered
it quickly. "Hello?"

"Kirsten? It's Erika Welby."

She stepped off the pathway and sat on an empty
park bench. "Oh. Hello."

"Am I calling at a bad time? Are you at work?"

"No, it's okay. I'm at lunch."

"I was wondering if you'd care to join us for dinner
again next Sunday?"

Care to? Since leaving the Welby house yesterday,
Kirsten had thought of countless more questions she
wished she'd asked.

"Before you answer," Erika continued, "I plan to
invite a few more people this time. I don't know if they'll
be able to come, but I want to ask. If it's all right with
you. And if you can come, of course."

"Who else did you want to ask?"

"Your fa—" She broke off, then continued, "Dallas
Hurst and his wife. And your grandfather and great-
grandmother."

My father.

At home last night, Kirsten had sat in the chair near
the phone, the directory open in her lap, images of her
father from Erika's photo album still fresh in her mind. She'd
discovered there were thirty Hursts listed in the Boise directory. Dallas Hurst wasn't one of them. When she'd called
information, she was told his number was unlisted.

"Kirsten?" Erika said. "Will you come?"

"I'll be there," she answered softly. "Can I bring anything?"

"There is one thing, if you don't mind."

Kirsten hoped the ingredients wouldn't cost too much or be too difficult to prepare.

"Do you have any photographs?"

"Sorry. What?"

"Photos, from when you were little."

"A few," she answered.

The Lundquists hadn't owned a camera while Kirsten was growing up. Her mother had always said she was going to buy one, but year after year went by and she never did. There was always something else they'd needed more. All Kirsten had were some school photos and a few snapshots taken by the mothers of friends.

"Bring them with you," Erika said. "Please."

"Okay. If I can find them. They're still in a box someplace."

"Well, if you can find them, then."

"Anything else?"

"No, just bring yourself. Come at one and we'll plan to eat at two."

"Okay."

"Good-bye, Kirsten. See you Sunday."

"Yeah. See you Sunday."

Kirsten pressed the End button, then realized there were tears in her eyes.

Photos. Photographs that showed her childhood, her life. Erika wanted to see them. But Kirsten realized she was

ashamed at what little she had to show compared to
Erika's large album. In addition to a number of snapshots
of Dallas Hurst with various members of the Welby
family, she'd seen photos of Ethan's growing-up years.
Ethan as a toddler. Ethan with a missing front tooth. Ethan
as the lead in a school play, wearing a ridiculous Sherlock
Holmes costume. Ethan playing golf with his dad. Ethan's
baptism, the boy surrounded by his family. Ethan on a trip
to Mexico with the youth from his church.

She couldn't help wondering what it might have
been like to see similar photos—photos of her—inside
Erika Welby's large album.

What if . . .

But Kirsten knew there were no answers to the
what-if's in life. It was better not to let herself wonder.

Chapter Twenty-Five

THE ANNUAL HURST FOURTH OF JULY celebration was its usual enormous success. The house and yard overflowed with people, drinks, and food. Paula was in her element, flirting and laughing with the men, gossiping with the women. Dallas played the crowd like a politician the week before an election. But in the end, after everyone was gone and the clean-up crew drove off with several pickup loads full of trash bags, Dallas was left feeling empty and low.

As he wandered through the house, checking the locks on the windows and doors before activating the security system, he wondered if he was merely exhausted or if what troubled him was the absence of the Welbys. They hadn't missed a Fourth at his house since the very first one.

Or maybe it was something else entirely. Something he couldn't quite put his finger on.

He supposed he could blame Kirsten Lundquist. If not for her unexpected appearance, things wouldn't be so tense between him and Paula. Nor would he be on the outs with his best friend in the world.

But he thought it was something more than that.

Lately, he hadn't taken the same pleasure in beating out his closest competitors for a new contract. He didn't feel the same excitement when faced with a new challenge. There just seemed to be something missing from his life.

Kids. He'd wanted kids of his own. He still did. But his gut told him even children wouldn't fill this strange void.

Maybe I'm just getting old.

Dallas climbed the stairs, deciding it might help his mood if he could resolve things with his wife.

He knew she wasn't asleep, although she pretended to be as he slipped into bed beside her. He could tell by the stiff set of her shoulders as she lay on her right side, her back turned toward him. He could tell by the forced steadiness of her breathing.

"Paula?"

No response.

He rolled onto his right side. "Paula, we need to talk."

Still nothing.

"I'm going to Steve and Erika's Sunday."

She held her breath.

"I want you to go with me."

"You're out of your mind."

He considered her comment for a few seconds, then said, "No, I'm not."

"This isn't right." She rolled onto her back, turning her head toward him. "Why can't you understand that?"

"Explain it to me."

She swore softly. "Why should I bother? It'll be like talking to a brick wall. You don't care what I think. My opinions don't matter. You've made up your mind, so go."

"I want you with me."

"No."

"Please. You're my wife. They're your friends."

"They're not my friends. They're yours. Erika hasn't ever liked me."

"Why would you say that?" He gently placed his hand on her shoulder.

She jerked away from him, turning onto her right side again, her rejection final.

Dallas stared at the ceiling.

Lately, being with Paula was like stepping into a deep freeze. He couldn't think of another time when things had been this bad between them. They'd had their share of ups and downs, sure. What couple didn't? But something told him this was different.

Maybe she was right. Maybe he shouldn't meet Kirsten.

But the girl claimed to be his daughter. His *daughter*, for crying out loud. He had to at least *meet* her, if only for curiosity's sake. Paula ought to be able to understand that.

What difference would it make to them in the long

run? It wasn't as though he were bringing home a toddler in diapers for Paula to raise. Kirsten was a grown woman. According to Erika, she had a job and a place to live. She didn't appear to be in Boise to make trouble. Erika promised the girl wasn't after his money, which seemed to be what Paula feared more than anything.

Anger began to replace worry.

He shouldn't have to justify his decisions. Paula was in the wrong. Let her act like a petulant child. He was going to do what he wanted, and she could like it or lump it. Two could play at this game.

⁓

Kirsten sat in a molded, hard plastic chair on her miniature deck, watching as three white ducks—like odd-shaped ghosts—waddled across the lawn toward one of the ponds that dotted the grounds. The fireworks had ended hours ago, and now the night air was cleansed of the smell of sulfur and smoke, replaced by the sweet scent of new-mown grass. A breeze tickled the tree limbs at the corner of her building.

She took a sip of iced tea, then lifted her gaze toward the starry sky. A sliver of moon rocked on its back directly overhead.

"I like it here," she whispered, as if to inform the celestial regions of her sentiments.

One of her most pleasant discoveries about Boise was how the temperature dropped quickly at nightfall. The low humidity was another plus, especially for a girl with naturally curly hair.

It's like I've come home.

That was fanciful thinking. "Home" wasn't part of a person's DNA, but it felt that way to Kirsten.

Her birth parents had grown up here. Idaho was in their blood, emotionally if not physiologically. They'd gone to the same schools and visited the same hangouts. They'd camped in the same mountains and swum in the same lakes and reservoirs. They'd floated the Boise River in inner tubes right into the heart of town, the same way Kirsten had seen others doing this week during her lunch-hour walks.

She wondered then if Dallas Hurst would come to Erika's on Sunday. Kirsten knew a little about him—but not enough to satisfy. Not nearly enough.

She sighed, took another sip of iced tea, then closed her eyes as she rested her head against the back of her chair.

Life was funny. She'd grown up thinking things would always go along the way they were, and then it all turned out different. She'd never dreamed of leaving Philadelphia, yet here she was, more than two thousand miles away, living in a much nicer apartment for a lot less rent. She'd met her birth mother and half brother. In a few days, she would meet her great-grandmother and her maternal grandfather. And if she got her heart's desire, she'd meet her biological father, too.

My dad.

Kirsten had been half of a family of two. But now . . .

Anticipation fluttered through her as she pictured herself in the center of a large gathering. Like one of those reunions people were always having with aunts and uncles and cousins, grandparents, siblings. The image was both wonderful and terrifying.

She opened her eyes again, gazing upward. The sky seemed endless, an inky canopy sprinkled with glitter.

If You're up there . . .

It wasn't a prayer. She couldn't say she believed or disbelieved in God. Almost everybody was spiritual in one way or another these days. She had one friend who went for past-life regression sessions at least once a month. A girl who'd worked in the next cubicle at her old office had talked about the angels that attended her, listening to her prayers.

Whatever makes you happy, I guess.

Then she thought about Erika and Ethan Welby, thought about some of the things they'd said and done in their few times together. They were . . . different. It was as though they had something she didn't have, or they knew something she didn't know.

Well, if You are up there, I'd like to think this will all play out okay in the end.

༄

Standing beside the bedroom window, Erika stared up at the starry heavens.

Father, what do I do now?

She could hear muted voices and music from the family room television. Steven was out there again, for the fourth night in a row. The first time he hadn't come to bed all night he'd used the excuse that he'd fallen asleep while watching TV. She'd believed him because she wanted to believe him.

She couldn't continue to pretend. The truth was her husband wouldn't even share the same bed with her anymore.

It seemed impossible that a marriage she'd thought sound and durable could go this wrong so quickly.

Marriage isn't supposed to be easy all the time. I know that, Lord. It isn't always hearts and flowers. I don't expect it to be. You never promised us smooth sailing, day in and day out. But Steven's forgotten that our marriage is supposed to be more than him just gritting his teeth and enduring me. God, how do I reach through the barricade of silence he's set up?

There was so much she longed to talk to Steven about. For over eighteen years, her husband had been her sounding board, her best and closest friend. She'd been able to talk to him about anything and everything. Well, everything with one exception. Now she wanted to tell him what she'd seen at the coffee shop on Monday so they could pray about it together. She wanted to tell him about her father's cold response to her confession. She wanted to pour out her fears and doubts, her hopes and dreams.

But she couldn't. Steven had removed himself from her.

I don't know what to do. She leaned her shoulder against the wall, the twinkling stars turning murky beyond her tears. *Everything seems so dark, Father, and I feel alone.*

Beloved.

She allowed the tears to fall.

I will guide you along the unfamiliar way. I will make the darkness bright before you and smooth out the road ahead of you.

She knew His voice. Knew it as certainly as she knew her own.

I will indeed do these things.

God had not forsaken her. In the darkness of this hour, she would cling to that promise for all she was worth.

CHAPTER TWENTY-SIX

DALLAS WAS TYING HIS SHOELACES the next
morning when Paula shuffled into the kitchen, looking
rumpled, sleepy, and beguiling. Beguiling enough to
forget last night's argument.

She gave him a cursory glance on her way to the
coffeemaker. "I don't suppose you've come to your senses,"
she mumbled.

Okay, maybe not that beguiling.

"You're being selfish, you know." She turned toward
him. "It isn't like you to think only of yourself."

That's because you expect me to think only of you. Isn't that
right, sweetheart?

She ran her fingers through her hair, then gave her
head an angry shake. "Why can't you see what you're
doing?" Her voice rose in pitch with each word. "*Why?*"

"I'm going for a run," he said, then left before his temper got the better of him.

A jogging path carried Dallas around the edge of a private park—empty on this Friday morning—and toward the river. The air was cool, but it held the promise of warmth.

Paula should be with me on Sunday when I meet Kirsten. She should choose to be with me.

His anger pounded in his chest the way his feet pounded the ground.

What if this girl is the only kid I'll ever have?

A sobering thought and not the first time it had drifted into his mind. If the doctor discovered that Paula was unable to conceive, it might be that there wouldn't be anyone to carry on after Dallas, no one to bear his name. Shouldn't a man have someone to leave everything to when he died?

Not that he meant to pass on any time soon.

Will I be ready when the time comes?

That was an unpleasant question, and the answer was simple: No, he wouldn't be ready. How could any man be ready for death?

I'll bet Steve is.

"Or at least he thinks he is," Dallas muttered, his breath coming faster.

But what if Steven and Erika were right? What if what they believed was more than superstitious nonsense? What if Dallas would be held accountable for all the not-so-nice things he'd done and the sometimes questionable choices he'd made?

It made a man wonder . . .

"Get a grip, Hurst," he said, louder this time. Then he lengthened his stride, as if trying to outrun his thoughts.

By the time he arrived home, he felt more like himself. He even felt calm enough to attempt smoothing things over with Paula, but she'd already left, so he showered, dressed, and headed for work. Halfway to the Hurst complex, he abruptly turned his car off the freeway and drove in another direction, steering along familiar streets and straight into the Welby driveway. He cut the engine and stared at the house.

What if they're right? The thought wouldn't leave him alone.

Steven and Erika had lived in this home for most of their marriage. They'd never had much in terms of material things. Dallas and Paula, on the other hand, always owned the latest gadgets, newest toys, fanciest cars, biggest house. Yet, as he sat there, the hot July sun beating down on the roof of his Lexus, he realized he envied Steven more than any man he knew. Even now, with this Kirsten matter going on, Dallas had a gut feeling the Welbys would be okay, when all was said and done. He didn't know if he could say the same for himself.

At that moment, Erika appeared through the gate to the backyard. She stopped when she saw Dallas, then lifted her hand in a half wave before walking down the drive, Motley at her heels.

Dallas opened the car door and got out.

"Steven isn't here," she said. "Did he know you were coming?"

"No. He wasn't expecting me. I just felt like dropping by."

She motioned with her head toward the backyard. "Come on back. I was having coffee on the patio."

"If I'm interrupting anything, I—"

"I'd be glad for the company, Dallas. The house feels a little empty this morning."

He followed her.

When they reached the patio, Erika asked, "How's Paula?"

"Mad."

"At you?"

"Me. You. The entire free English-speaking world." He sank onto a chair.

Erika sat opposite him. "About Kirsten? Or is there . . . something else?"

Dallas raked the fingers of his right hand through his hair. "Mostly. But I'm beginning to think it goes deeper than that."

A frown creased Erika's forehead, and Dallas wondered what she was thinking.

After a lengthy silence, he said, "Sometimes I don't even know who Paula is."

"She's your wife."

He grunted.

"Nobody ever claimed marriage was easy," Erika said softly, her gaze dropping to the Bible on the table.

"So how does a couple make it work? How are you and Steven making it work in the middle of this mess?"

She offered him an uncertain smile. "I'm trusting Jesus to bring us through."

"Jesus . . ." He knew, even as he said the name, that this was why he'd come. "That's always your answer, isn't it? Yours and Steve's."

"He's the only answer I know."

"I've never understood what you two mean when you say stuff like that," Dallas said honestly.

She was quiet for a short while, then said, "I'll try to explain if you care to listen."

"Okay. I'm listening."

It wasn't as if Erika and Steven had never shared the gospel message with Dallas before. But this time, something was different. This time, Dallas didn't just listen to what Erika had to say. This time he *heard*.

God loved him.

Jesus died for him.

The truth overwhelmed him. It surrounded him, invaded him, transformed him.

He believed, and suddenly everything had changed.

Dallas lifted his gaze to stare at Erika. "I feel . . . it's like . . . I don't know. I can't explain it."

"You're a new person inside, new in your spirit."

"Yes." Dallas nodded. "That's what I feel—like someone new. It's too simple, isn't it?"

She smiled. "First Corinthians 1:18 says—" she quickly flipped open the Bible on the table and read the verse aloud—"'I know very well how foolish the message of the cross sounds to those who are on the road to destruction. But we who are being saved recognize this message as the very power of God.'"

Dallas wondered if he should ask Erika to come to his house to talk to Paula. If she explained it all the same way she had to him, then maybe Paula would believe, too.

"Steven and Ethan will be thrilled when they hear what happened today."

"You've all been praying for this for a long time." It wasn't a question. Dallas knew it was true.

"A long time."

He stood. "I'd better go." He took a step back from the table, then asked, "What time's church on Sunday, and how do I get there?"

ॐ

The instant Erika saw Steven's car pulling into the driveway, she rushed outside.

"You'll never guess what happened," she said before he was out of the car. "Dallas came over. He . . . Steven, he accepted Christ."

Her husband's eyes widened. "He what?"

"It's true." She nodded. "He did. About six hours ago. We were in the backyard and he let me tell him about the Lord, and then we prayed together and he asked Jesus into his heart."

Steven turned away, grabbing a duffel bag off the backseat, then closing the car door. When he turned again, he said, "Are you sure he wasn't doing it to pacify you?"

This wasn't the reaction she'd imagined. "Of course, I'm sure."

"How long was he here?"

"I . . . I didn't pay any attention. It seemed like no time at all."

A shadow passed across her husband's face. "Time flies when you're having fun."

She drew back, stung by the rancor in his words.

"I need something to eat," Steven said and started toward the house.

She wanted to make him stop, wanted to make him talk to her, to tell her what he was thinking, what he was feeling. But she didn't know how to make him do anything. She didn't know what to say to him. She used to know. She used to be able to read his thoughts, to know what the next words out of his mouth would be.

But no longer.

Oh, Steven, what's happened to us?

Heavyhearted, Erika followed him inside.

$\backsim$

It was after midnight.

Steven reclined in his easy chair, the television flickering at him from the opposite wall, the volume turned low. So low he couldn't hear. It didn't matter. He wasn't listening anyway.

Erika had led Dallas to Christ. The news should have caused rejoicing. They were celebrating in heaven. But not here. Not in this room.

Enmity burned in Steven's heart the way bile burned a person's throat, hot and sour. He resented Dallas, and no amount of prayer could change his feelings.

What prayer?

No, he hadn't prayed. He hadn't opened his Bible in days either. When he was with other believers, he put on a practiced Christian facade and mouthed all the right words, while on the inside, the worms of jealousy and hatred ate at his soul.

Steven knew he'd slipped away from the Lord, knew he was slipping still, knew he was the one who could change it if he wanted. But he didn't take that first step. Couldn't or wouldn't made no difference. He simply didn't.

"You'll never guess what happened. Dallas came over. He . . . Steven, he accepted Christ."

He ground his teeth at the memory of Erika's words. He didn't believe his friend's spiritual rebirth was real, no matter what Erika said. Deep down—in that small, secret corner of his heart—he didn't think Dallas was worthy of God's forgiveness. Not yet. Steven wanted him to suffer first.

Everything always came easy to Dallas. Everything. He'd played the bachelor for years, escorting a parade of beautiful women to parties and political functions. He'd built a successful business and made a small fortune with what seemed very little effort. He'd lived a charmed life, no doubt about it.

But Dallas also had betrayed Steven as cruelly as any man could betray another, and now he was going to be forgiven by God for his sins. As easy as that.

It wasn't just, and Steven wanted justice.

Or maybe what he wanted was revenge.

"Dad? You still up?"

Steven glanced toward the hall entrance where Ethan now stood. "How was the movie?" he asked.

"Okay. Cammi liked it more than I did." Ethan walked into the family room and sat on the couch, fixing his eyes on his father, a frown pinching his brow.

Steven turned his gaze toward the TV. "You probably should get to bed. You work the morning shift, don't you?"

"What's going on between you and Mom?"

"Nothing that you need to worry about."

"I'm not blind, Dad."

The television continued to flicker, and Steven continued to stare at it, unseeing.

"I don't think you're being fair to Mom."

The words were spoken softly, solemnly, but they slid between Steven's defenses like a sharp knife between his ribs, piercing him, shaming him.

"She needs you."

Steven rubbed a hand over his face. "I can't talk about this now."

"Don't you think you should—"

"I don't need to be lectured by my son," Steven snapped, looking at Ethan again. "You don't understand everything, so just let it alone."

Ethan's gaze didn't waver. "I understand plenty." He stood. "What about doing the *right* thing? What about loving somebody even when it isn't easy to love them?"

"Ethan," he warned.

"It's time to step up to the plate, Dad." With those words, he left the room.

Steven remained stubbornly in his chair, only the flickering set and his anger for company.

CHAPTER TWENTY-SEVEN

THE CONGREGATION STOOD as the worship team played one of Erika's favorite praise songs. Around her, voices and arms were raised as others declared to the Lord, "You are in control."

Erika bowed her head and closed her eyes. *It doesn't feel like You're in control, God. I need to hear Your voice. I need to hear Your promises again.*

Steven hadn't come to church today. When Erika and Ethan left the house, Steven was still sitting in the family-room easy chair, the same place he'd spent every night for the past week.

"You are in control," the congregation sang on.

To her right stood proof that God could bring good from all things. Dallas had found Christ after a decade of

closing his ears to the truth they'd shared with him.
Wasn't that reason enough for hope?

But her husband wasn't here.

She opened her eyes, lifted her head, looked at the
cross behind the altar.

Jesus . . . .

She felt a hand alight on her shoulder. Turning her
head, she saw Barb Dobson.

"Let's go pray," Barb said softly.

Erika nodded.

She allowed her friend to lead her to the altar rail-
ing where they knelt between others. Barb placed an arm
around Erika's shoulders, then leaned close and began to
pray. She asked God for wisdom. She asked God to
accomplish His will. She asked God to heal old wounds
and to bring something new to life.

Yes, Lord, Erika's heart cried again and again. *Yes,
Lord. Yes.*

She felt someone else kneel at her right side and
place a hand over hers. She opened her eyes to see who
it was.

Ethan.

That was when she began to weep.

❧

The demons of jealousy and resentment taunted Steven
as he wandered the silent house.

"Dallas is coming to church," Erika had told him.
"You should be there."

But he hadn't gone. He couldn't go. Didn't want to go.

So he imagined them instead. Erika, Dallas, and Ethan sitting in *his* pew, looking like a family.

Did Erika ever wish she'd married Dallas instead of him? It was possible. After all, Dallas was successful. He was rich. He'd made something of himself. If Erika had told Dallas she was pregnant, he probably would have married her. It could have been Erika living in that large house instead of Paula. Ethan might have been Dallas's son instead of his.

She could've had an easy life with him. She must have thought about it over the years. She must have wondered if she made the right choice.

He stopped his pacing in the kitchen. Evidence of preparation for the afternoon's barbecue was everywhere. Paper plates and napkins were on the counter, along with plastic forks and knives. Outside on the patio, the table had been covered with a red-and-white-checked cloth.

Erika had arranged for Kirsten to meet her maternal grandfather and great-grandmother here today. Most significantly, she'd arranged for Kirsten to meet Dallas. Kirsten's father. Right here in Steven's home. Right under his nose. Whether he liked it or not.

⁓

Erika set her purse and Bible on the kitchen counter. She felt stronger than she had when she left for church. She felt bolstered by prayer and the support of her friends and her son. She knew she couldn't pretend that things would get better between her and Steven without their facing the problem head-on. She had to make him see that, too.

She found her husband sitting on the bed, tying his shoes. He glanced up when she entered, then looked down again.

She closed the door and leaned against it. "We can't go on like this, Steven."

He got up and disappeared into the walk-in closet, acting as if he hadn't heard her.

She raised her voice. "I mean it. We've *got* to talk."

"Can't it wait?" He stepped into the closet doorway. "I've got to fire up the grill. We've got company coming. Remember?" His voice was hard, his expression the same. "You're the one who invited them."

"This is more important."

"I don't feel like talking right now, Erika."

"We can't go on like this. You can't keep treating me this way. You can't keep treating Dallas this way either."

"I don't want to talk about Dallas." He disappeared into the closet a second time.

"Well, I *do*!" She strode across the room. "I *do* want to talk about him. And about you. And about us." Tears threatened, and she paused to fight them back. "What is it you want, Steven? Blood?"

He faced her, and for a moment, she thought he might admit blood was precisely what he wanted.

He said, "I'm doing the best I can."

"No." She sniffed. "No, you're not."

"Let it go, Erika."

"You don't want to touch me. You never kiss me or tell me you love me. You walk wide circles around me. Like I'm a leper or something. How long do you plan to sleep in your easy chair? The rest of our lives?" Loneliness pressed in on her, crushing her. She lifted a hand toward him. "Please—"

He swore softly. Steven *never* swore. Erika stepped backward as if he'd struck her.

"I can't help what I feel," he snapped. He exited the closet, giving her a wide berth on his way toward the door.

"Steven—"

Stopping, he swore again. "Let it go. Okay?"

"No," she whispered.

He turned to face her. "No what?"

"No, it isn't okay. No, I won't let it go."

He glowered at her.

"You're not doing the best you can, Steven. You could change if you wanted to. You just don't want to."

"I haven't left you, have I?"

The room seemed to grow smaller, the air thinner, as the two of them stared at each other.

Erika broke the silence. "Maybe you should."

His eyes narrowed. "Maybe I will."

Who are you, Steven? What's become of the man I've loved? Where's he hiding?

"Do you *want* me to leave?" he asked, the hard edge gone from his voice for the first time.

I don't know what I want. I don't know what to do. I don't know what's right or wrong, up or down, in or out. All I know is that I want you to love me. I want you to touch me the way you used to. I want you to kiss me on the mouth and remember that you're my husband. I want you to act like the man I've known and loved for over half of my life.

"Well, I guess I've got my answer." He headed for the closet again. "I'll pack a few things and get out of your way."

That's not my answer, she wanted to cry. *Don't go, Steven. Don't leave.*

But she couldn't seem to speak.

And he couldn't seem to stay.

Chapter Twenty-Eight

No unfamiliar cars were in the driveway, Kirsten noted as she walked toward the front door. She was either the first to arrive . . . or no one else was coming.

Before Kirsten could ring the bell, the door opened, revealing Erika.

"Hi." Erika's smile was more nervous than happy. "Glad you could come."

Kirsten nodded, wondering when—or if—this awkwardness between them would go away.

"I hope you're hungry. I've fixed four different salads, and we've got steaks ready to go on the grill."

She's my mom, and she's doing all of this for me.

Kirsten felt an odd pleasure at the thought, followed by a sting of guilt. From the beginning of her search, she'd been determined not to dishonor the mother who'd raised her by sharing that title with Erika Welby.

And yet . . .

"Come in." Erika stepped back into the house. "I hope you remembered the photos. Did you?"

"Yes. I found a few." She pulled a small envelope from the side pocket of her purse.

"May I?" Erika held out a hand.

With a nod, Kirsten passed them to her.

Erika opened the envelope and withdrew the photos. She looked at the first one, staring at it for a long time before asking, "How old were you here?"

"Six. It's my first-grade school picture."

"You look a little like Ethan did at the same age."

"Really?" Kirsten stepped to Erika's side and studied the photograph.

"Look at your cowlick. Ethan's got one in the exact same spot."

"I never noticed his."

"Well, it was more obvious before he cut his hair so short." She smiled. "You both inherited it from me."

Kirsten raised her eyes to Erika's hairline. "I always hated it." The instant the words were out of her mouth, she regretted them.

But Erika laughed softly. "Me, too." As naturally as if she'd been doing it for years, she hooked her arm through Kirsten's. "Let's look at the rest in the kitchen where the light's better."

The sound of a closing car door stopped them before they took their first step. Kirsten's heart seemed to stop, too. Then it raced like an engine with the throttle stuck at full bore.

Erika released Kirsten's arm and moved to the door, opening it again.

Kirsten saw the car, a pale gold Lexus convertible—the kind that cost more than she made in an entire year, maybe two. The dark-haired man standing beside it was good-looking, well dressed, and . . . and her father. She recognized him from the snapshots she'd seen in Erika's album.

"He came," she whispered.

Erika placed her arm around Kirsten's shoulders. "He came." She gently guided Kirsten onto the front porch.

A second car pulled into the drive, this one a long, four-door "boat" with fins instead of fenders. Straight out of the sixties, the automobile's burgundy paint was faded, the white vinyl top cracked and peeling.

"That's your grandfather and your great-grandmother. My mother's mother."

Kirsten's heart was pounding so hard she almost couldn't hear what Erika said.

Dallas Hurst had obviously noticed the new arrivals, too. With a long, easy stride, he moved to the passenger side of the Olds and opened the door, then leaned forward and assisted an elderly woman from the car.

Louisa Scott had a short cap of silver hair. She was tiny—no more than five-two and a hundred pounds—and her smile was made more obvious by the bright lipstick she wore. She reached up and patted Dallas's cheek, as if he were a schoolboy rather than a man in his forties.

Kirsten shifted her gaze toward the driver's side of the automobile where her maternal grandfather now stood.

Trevor James was a tall, slender man but somewhat stooped in the shoulders. His hair, what he had of it, was stone gray. And he was definitely *not* smiling as he stared toward the front porch.

"Hi, Dad," Erika called. "Grams." She hesitated another moment before adding, "Hi, Dallas."

The newly arrived trio walked toward the house, Louisa Scott between the two men.

"I hope you brought good appetites," Erika said, "because we've got lots of food."

Kirsten's nerves screeched as she waited for the moment of introduction. She wasn't sure where to look. At her father? her grandfather? her great-grandmother? the ground? the sky?

From the doorway behind her, there came a most welcome voice. "They're all here." A moment later, Ethan stepped to her other side. Kirsten looked at her half brother. He grinned back at her, a twinkle of encouragement in his dark blue eyes. "They won't bite," he whispered. "Not even Grandpa."

Amazingly enough, she believed him.

She does *look like me.*

Any lingering doubt in Dallas's mind about the girl's parentage vanished the instant he laid eyes on her.

238

"Everybody," Erika said, a slight quaver in her voice, "this is Kirsten. Kirsten," Erika continued, "this is . . . your grandfather, Trevor James."

If Trevor said one unkind word, Dallas would flatten him, old man or not. So help him, he would.

A hesitant smile curved the corners of Kirsten's mouth as she nodded toward the older man.

"And this is Grams."

Kirsten repeated the nod, but that wasn't good enough for Louisa Scott. She moved up the steps, unaided by either of the men, and embraced the girl.

"Praise the Lord." Louisa didn't let her diminutive height stop her. With hands on Kirsten's shoulders, she pulled her great-granddaughter down so she could kiss her cheek. "How glad I am you're here." She kissed Kirsten's other cheek. "You're the picture of loveliness, my dear. The very picture of loveliness."

"Thank you."

Erika motioned toward Dallas. "And this . . . is your father."

He hadn't anticipated the lump in his throat or the heaviness in his chest. He couldn't have spoken, not if his life depended on it.

"Hello," Kirsten said, her voice scarcely audible.

This was his daughter. She was a part of him, a part of his blood. There was something primal in the way that made him feel. There was a sense of pride, too, as if he'd done something unique in helping to give her life. But there was something more besides. Something . . .

"For cryin' out loud," Trevor James snapped, "are we going to stand out here all day or can we go in?"

Dallas was almost grateful for the interruption. He needed a bit of time to sort through these foreign emotions.

～

As Erika motioned her guests inside, she fought hard to maintain her thin veneer of control.

A few hours. I'll be okay for a few hours. Then I can fall apart.

"Mom, where's Dad?" Ethan asked softly.

"He had to leave." She met her son's gaze and forced a smile. "I'll need you to grill the steaks. Okay?"

"Sure, but—"

"We'd better hurry. You know how your grand-father gets when he's hungry." She followed after the others.

If I stay busy, I'll be okay. I won't think about Steven. I won't think about it yet. Not yet.

But of course she *did* think about it. Her husband of eighteen years had left her. The man she'd loved since she was fifteen had walked out of her life. How could she not think about it?

God, how did we come to this?

Her guests moved outside onto the patio. Fortu-nately, the temperature was cooler than it had been in recent weeks, and there was a pleasant breeze coming from the west. While Erika watched from the kitchen window, ostensibly getting things ready for their meal, she observed Grams sit down beside Kirsten on the picnic-table bench. She immediately took hold of the girl's hand and patted it affectionately. Erika's father sat on the opposite side of the patio. Dallas went to stand with Ethan at the grill.

Was it worth it? Was having them all here worth losing her husband?

She closed her eyes and pressed the heels of her hands against the edge of the sink, supporting herself, her knees weak.

Father, what shall I do? I'm frightened. Was it wrong to want to know my daughter? Was it too much to ask of Steven?

"Erika? Are you all right?"

She straightened and looked toward Dallas, standing in the doorway. "Yes," she lied, "I'm fine."

"Ethan said Steve had to go out."

She nodded.

Dallas entered the kitchen. "It's because I'm here, isn't it?"

She shook her head, then nodded.

"I shouldn't have come." He glanced outside, his gaze settling on Kirsten. His voice dropped. "She's beautiful, Erika."

"Yes, she is."

He was silent for several moments before he said, "Paula wouldn't come because she still thinks Kirsten's after our money or something."

Maybe Paula's absence had to do with Kirsten, but Erika doubted it. She thought it had more to do with Warren Carmichael and knowing that Erika had seen

them together. She turned and walked to the refrigerator, afraid her face would give something away. She
couldn't deal with another crisis right now.

"Can I help you with anything?" Dallas asked.

She took the platter of meat from the refrigerator.
"You can take these to Ethan. Then you can go over and
talk to Kirsten. That's why you're here. To get to know
your daughter."

He gave her a guilty smile, took the platter, and left
the kitchen.

*Don't think about anything. Don't think about Steven or
Paula. I can get through this. I can. I can. I can.*

‹›

Dallas was a master at small talk, of putting people at ease
in awkward situations, of knowing just the right thing to
say at just the right moment. But for some reason, that
talent failed him today. He didn't know what to say to this
young woman who was his daughter. Thank goodness for
Ethan.

With everyone seated around the table, the blessing
spoken, Ethan said, "Tell us about your trip across the
country. Anything exciting happen?"

Kirsten shook her head. "Not really, although I did
begin to feel a kinship with burly truckers in T-shirts and
baseball caps. It seemed like I ate every meal with them."

"And your new job?" Louisa asked. "How do you
like it?"

"I think I'm going to like it a lot." Kirsten smiled at

her great-grandmother. "But I'm still feeling a bit lost and out of place."

Louisa nodded. "God does His best work in us when we're feeling out of place. I'm sure He has something wonderful in store for you, dearest."

"I suppose," Kirsten replied, her gaze lowering to the food on her plate.

"Isn't Steven going to join us?" Trevor demanded abruptly.

Dallas glanced toward Erika and thought she looked unusually pale.

"I . . . I told you, Dad. He had to go out."

"Well, where would he have to go on a Sunday afternoon, for pete's sake?"

"I'm not sure. It was . . . he had to leave rather suddenly." She grabbed the bowl on the table in front of her and offered it to Dallas. "More potato salad?"

"Thanks," he answered, taking it, even though he hadn't yet touched the salad already on his plate.

Dallas could see Erika was trying hard not to show how upset she was by Steven's absence. He was pretty sure nobody at the table was fooled by her efforts.

Once again, it was Ethan who came to the rescue. "Tell us about Philadelphia. What was it like growing up there? I mean, think of it. That's where the Liberty Bell is. All that history. It must be great getting to see those places where our nation got its start."

For the remainder of the meal, Kirsten politely answered the questions that were posed to her. Dallas thought he might have learned as much about her life by what she didn't say as by what she did. More than once he wondered what might have been if he'd had the chance to raise her. And several times he felt a strange sense of awe at the recurrent thought: *I'm her father. I'm a dad.*

He was thinking that very thing when Trevor suddenly announced it was time he took Louisa home. It didn't take long for the farewells to be spoken. The next thing he knew, Dallas found himself alone on the patio with Kirsten. Erika and Ethan had disappeared into the house, cleaning up.

Kirsten looked at him, then at her watch. "I suppose I should leave, too."

"So soon?"

"Tomorrow starts another workweek."

"I . . . ah . . . I thought we might talk awhile longer. Just the two of us."

She looked at him with eyes so like his own that it was spooky.

"You've answered questions all afternoon," he said. "I thought you might want to ask a few questions yourself."

"Questions about what?"

"Well . . . about me, I guess."

Kirsten drew a deep breath. "There is one thing."

"What's that?"

"I'd like to know where I'm going to fit into your life."

Where does she fit in? It was a good question.

He remembered Paula's words: *"Don't you get it? She'll be after our money. Just you wait and see."*

Paula wasn't about to make Kirsten feel welcome,

and if he pursued a relationship with his newfound daughter, his wife would make his life agony.

"I know," Kirsten said, interrupting the lengthy silence. "It's complicated. Right?"

He nodded. "Yes, I guess it is. But don't take that to mean I don't want you to be a part of it."

"You do?"

The vulnerability revealed in those two small words shook him to the core.

"Yes," he answered, "I do."

He was rewarded with a smile that would have melted any father's heart.

Exhaustion settled over Erika like a heavy cloak, and yet she couldn't sit still. After Dallas and Kirsten finally left and Ethan went over to Cammi's to watch a video, there was plenty of tidying up to do. But when all of the obvious chores were done, she found herself making work in order to stay busy. The house was too silent, too empty, now that she was alone again.

As dusk turned to night she went outside and sank onto a patio chair, listening to the crickets' evening serenade. It wasn't long before Motley joined her. She stroked his head, thankful for a warm body to touch, thankful to feel connected to something living and breathing.

She'd read once that babies could die if they were never held. They needed to be touched.

So do I.

The reality of Steven's departure hit her like a sledgehammer, and she began to cry. She cried as she hadn't been able to cry since the moment he left. The tears came silently, copiously, rolling down her cheeks and dropping onto her bare arms in an unending stream.

What am I going to do? How could you do this, Steven? How could you do this to us?

JANUARY 1984

Erika stared at her reflection in the mirror of the hotel suite's bathroom. She was wearing a white, frothy negligee, a bridal-shower gift from Anna Smith. A nightgown worthy of an innocent, blushing bride on her wedding night. But she wasn't innocent, was she?

Terror seized her. When Steven made love to her, would he know the truth? Would he be able to guess?

Beyond the bathroom door, her groom awaited her. Soon he would carry her to that king-size bed. Soon he would claim her for his own.

Oh, Steven, I'm sorry. I love you. Please don't know. Please don't guess. It seems so long ago now, like it happened to somebody else.

She drew a deep breath, steadying her nerves.

We're going to have a wonderful life. I'm going to be the best, most loving wife any man ever had. I'll never let you regret marrying me. Never, never, never. I promise.

A light tap sounded on the door. "Erika? You okay in there?"

She drew another shaky breath, then turned from the mirror. "Yes, Steven. I . . . I'm fine. I'll be right out."

Please don't know. Please love me forever. Please.

Chapter Twenty-Nine

Erika couldn't remember a longer, more sleepless night than the one just past. She'd been tortured by countless doubts and fears, her thoughts run amuck.

The morning held little promise for improvement. She knew she must tell Ethan about his father. Her son would have seen that Steven's car was absent when he returned from Cammi's last night. She'd avoided his questions by retiring before he got home. She wouldn't be able to avoid them this morning.

How would she find the words to tell him? How could she explain what had happened when she didn't understand it herself? Ethan adored his father. They'd always been close. He'd trusted his parents to stay together, to honor their wedding vows, to cleave to each other as the Bible said they should.

Guilt and anger warred within her. Guilt for what *she'd* done. Anger for what *he'd* done.

If she hadn't said the things she'd said . . . If he'd had one ounce of forgiveness in him . . . If she hadn't kept the truth from him all these years . . . If he'd thought about her and not just himself . . .

She got out of bed, slipped on her robe, and went to make a pot of coffee.

Ethan was seated at the kitchen table, waiting for her.

"Where's Dad?" he asked the moment their eyes met.

She stopped. Her throat tightened. "I don't know."

"He walked out on us?"

"Not us." She moved to the table and sat on one of the chairs. "Me. He feels betrayed. He needs some time to work it through."

"And he's not betraying you now?" Her son's voice rose, and his eyes lit with anger. "Don't make excuses for him, Mom. He's acting like a jerk."

Erika shook her head slowly. "Don't say things like that about your father."

"Why not, if it's true?"

"Because it isn't respectful."

"Maybe he doesn't deserve any respect right now."

"Ethan," she whispered, fighting another wave of tears. "Don't."

"I can't help it, Mom. All my life I've listened to him telling me I need to do the right thing, even when it isn't the easy thing. He's said we're supposed to forgive others, no matter what they've done. But he's not forgiving you, is he? And you're the first person he ought to forgive.

You've always stood by him and prayed for him and just been there when you were needed."

"I shouldn't have kept Kirsten a secret."

Ethan made a rude sound. "Stop making excuses for him."

"I never—"

"You deserve better than this, Mom." He stood. "And so do I."

Erika didn't fight the tears any longer. She let them fall.

Her son looked as if he was fighting tears of his own. "We'll be okay," he said thickly. "I'll take care of you."

꒳

Kirsten stood beneath the shower, eyes closed, the water pulsing against her scalp. She'd slept fitfully and felt more exhausted now than she had when she'd gone to bed. Not her favorite way to start the workweek.

She wondered if her father had slept any better.

Where do I fit in? Am I going to be like a real daughter or only a casual acquaintance?

At least Dallas hadn't made her feel like a mere mistake from his past. To be honest, she'd liked him, and she thought he might like her, too.

She turned off the water. The bathroom was thick with steam, the mirror fogged.

Half an hour later, with her hair blown dry and her makeup applied, Kirsten returned to the bedroom to dress. She was almost done when the phone rang.

"Hello."

"Hi, honey."

Kirsten sat on the edge of the bed, cradling the phone between ear and shoulder as she reached for her shoes. "Hi, Mom."

"I know you must be getting ready for work," Donna said, "but I'm dying to know how it went yesterday. Did you meet Mr. Hurst?"

"Yes, I met him. It went good."

"What's he like?"

Kirsten knew she was on thin ice. Her mother was putting on a good front, trying hard to be supportive, but she was still afraid of losing her daughter.

She chose her words carefully. "He's nice. Good-looking. He's got his own company. He's married, but I haven't met his wife. She wasn't there yesterday."

Her mother was silent for a few moments, then said, "Have you heard from Van?"

"No. Why?"

"Mrs. Mendoza from up the street thinks he's got a new girlfriend."

"He's a nice guy. Girls like him," Kirsten said.

"I thought he'd wait to see if you came back."

"I didn't want him to wait, Mom."

"You seemed to like him a lot. I thought—"

"I did like him." Kirsten sighed. "But we weren't destined for anything permanent. I think we both knew that from the start."

Her mother changed the subject again. "Did I tell you I might get a puppy?"

"Really?"

Donna Lundquist had never been big on pets.

"One of my regulars has a dog with a new litter, and she offered me one of the puppies. Says it'll be good company now that you've moved away and I'm all alone."

Kirsten felt the required sting of guilt. "What kind of dog is it?"

"Heinz 57, but small. A kind of terrier." Her mother sighed, then said, "Guess I'd better hang up now. I know you need to get to work."

Kirsten glanced at the clock. "Yes, I do." She stood. "Let me know if you get that puppy."

"I will. I love you, honey."

"I love you, too, Mom. Bye."

She placed the phone in its cradle and was surprised to find her vision blurred by tears.

Why, she wondered, did life have to be so complicated?

~

Steven had spent a sleepless night on the small sofa in his office at the school. He cleaned himself up in the morning in the boys' washroom.

What are you doing here? he asked himself as he stared into the thigh-high sink, the faucet dripping.

He'd replayed the scene in their bedroom yesterday a hundred times, trying to make it come out differently, but it always ended the same—with his leaving.

Would he have changed things if he could? He

wasn't sure. Didn't he have a right to be angry? Didn't he have a right to want someone to pay for the hurt and anger he was feeling? Well, didn't he?

No, a small, unwelcome voice whispered in his heart. *No, you don't have the right.*

Steven chose to ignore his conscience. He turned and left the washroom.

Since he didn't want his secretary to know he'd spent the night at the school, he decided now would be a good time to go get something to eat. In his office, he grabbed his duffel bag off the floor, then headed outside to his car.

After he had breakfast, he'd need to find a place to stay, he thought as he tossed his bag onto the passenger seat and slid behind the wheel. The thought chilled him. He hadn't lived alone since his college days.

Go home, that persistent little voice said, but he shut his ears to it.

He was the wronged party here, and he wasn't going home.

CHAPTER THIRTY

TO DALLAS'S SURPRISE, the days immediately
following the gathering at Steven and Erika's home were
better than those immediately before. Paula was loving,
affectionate, and agreeable from sunup until well after
sundown. She even offered to have Kirsten over to the
house for dinner so they could become acquainted. Dallas
wasn't sure what had brought about his wife's change of
heart, but he was glad for it. Now if he could make things
right between him and Steven, all would be perfect.

When his secretary buzzed to tell him he had a call
on line four, he hoped it was Steven returning one of the
several messages he'd left at the school this week. It wasn't.

"Dallas, this is Nick Franklin. I'm the youth pastor at
Harvest Fellowship. Ethan introduced us last Sunday."

"Yes. I remember."

"Ethan told me you're a new believer. He thought you might be interested in the men's Bible study we have on Thursday mornings. Steven Welby's a regular. We hoped you might join us tomorrow."

A number of excuses popped into his head: He usually ran a few miles on weekday mornings. He was too busy at work to add another thing to his schedule. He doubted Steven would be overjoyed to see him there.

In the end, he said, "Sure. I think I can make it. When and where do you meet?"

Pastor Nick gave him the time—six o'clock—and the name of the restaurant; then the two men said good-bye and hung up.

Me in a Bible study. Who'd've believed it?

Dallas shook his head, then glanced at the clock. It was approaching the lunch hour. He walked out of his office, stopping at his secretary's desk. "Where's the clos-est store where I can buy a Bible?"

The surprised look on Karla's face was almost comi-cal. Or maybe it was tragic. After she recovered herself, she looked up the nearest Christian bookstore in the phone book, wrote the address on a slip of paper, and handed it to him.

On his drive across town, he pondered his secre-tary's reaction. He couldn't help wondering how his coworkers, acquaintances, and friends would describe him if asked. Several words sprang to mind.

Driven.

Ambitious.

Greedy.

He winced. Surely there were a few complimentary words that could be added to that list. He was *successful*. He was a *good provider*. He was as *honest* as any other businessman he knew.

Something told him God wasn't impressed.

꒰

On her lunch hour, Kirsten took a blanket to the riverbank and spread it on the ground in the shade of a large, gnarly tree. Then she removed her shoes and stuck her bare feet in the cold water while eating her sandwich and sipping a diet soda. The tree limbs stirred overhead, causing shadow and light to sway around and over her.

But the soothing sounds of rippling water and fluttering leaves couldn't work their magic, not with the thoughts that troubled her mind.

She'd learned last night that Steven Welby had moved out of his house. What Erika hadn't said—but what Kirsten knew—was that she was the reason.

"I'm sorry," she'd told her birth mother, feeling how lame those words were.

"It isn't your fault. Don't think it is."

Kirsten hadn't replied. What, after all, could she have said?

She lay back on the blanket and stared at the patch of blue sky beyond the branches. She wondered how Ethan was taking his father's leaving. It had to be a tough blow. He was a pretty together kid, but still. Would he blame her?

Probably. And why not? If she hadn't dropped suddenly into the middle of their family—

Nearby, she heard a man clear his throat. She sat up, startled.

Dallas Hurst smiled sheepishly. "Sorry. Didn't mean to give you a scare."

"You didn't."

He could have called her a liar. He let his smile broaden instead. "Mind if I join you?"

She shook her head, feeling as nervous as she had when they'd first met.

He sank onto the edge of her blanket. "Sorry I haven't gotten around to calling you this week."

She shrugged her shoulders, as if she hadn't counted the hours that had passed since Sunday.

"I stopped by your office, and they told me I could find you down here." He gazed at the river. "Good place to unwind and reflect."

"I've thought so."

Dallas looked at her again. "Paula, my wife, would like you to come to dinner on Friday. If you don't already have other plans."

She didn't, but—

"Paula's had a hard time adjusting to the thought of me having a daughter your age."

"I've been a big surprise to everybody."

"No kidding."

"A bad surprise or a good one?" She hadn't meant to ask that question. The words slipped out of their own accord. And once spoken, she was scared to death of his answer.

Her father's dark eyes narrowed slightly as he watched her. It seemed an eternity before he replied, "A little of both, I guess."

Was she glad for his honesty or hurt by the truth?

"Unexpected change isn't usually welcomed with open arms," he added.

"No," she sighed, "I suppose not."

He peered at the river. "There've been a number of changes in my life recently. Changes I hadn't planned on. I haven't handled all of them well, but I'm working on it." He was silent for a few moments; then he continued, his voice low and pensive. "On Sunday, you asked where you fit into my life. I didn't give you an answer."

Kirsten found it hard to breathe.

"I'd like to learn to be your father." Dallas looked at her again. "I've had no practice at being a dad. Paula and I've wanted to start a family, but it hasn't happened yet. I'll probably make lots of mistakes as we get to know each other. But that's what I'd like, if it's what you want, too."

It was what she'd come to Idaho for—to find a father, *her* father. Oh, there'd been her job, but that had been a means to an end. What she'd wanted for more years than she could count was to have a father's love. Was it possible that her dream was within her grasp?

She nodded, fighting the lump in her throat. "I'd like it, too."

"Terrific." He grinned.

Kirsten released a nervous laugh. "Terrific."

"About Friday," he said as he glanced at his wristwatch. "How about six o'clock for dinner?"

"Sure."

"I'll call Erika and Steve and ask them to join us. You'll feel more comfortable if they—"

"You don't know?" Kirsten felt a little sick to her stomach.

"Know what?"

"He's moved out."

"Who?" Dallas stared at her, wide-eyed. "*Steve?*"

She nodded. "I found out last night. He left on Sunday before the barbecue. Erika didn't say anything then because she didn't want to spoil things for . . . for us."

"Not this." Her father rubbed a hand over his face. "Not to them. Not Steve and Erika."

Erika let the newspaper fall closed on the table.

"What am I to do?" she whispered.

She had no idea where to begin looking for work. It was a lifetime ago since she'd held a paying job. How many employers counted "Den Mother" as a marketable skill or "Volunteer Teacher's Assistant" as previous work experience?

She hadn't heard a word from Steven in the past three days, and the pain of his absence was nearly more than she could bear. Worse still was seeing Ethan's bewilderment and anger.

Would Steven have left, she wondered guiltily, if she hadn't said he should? Could they have worked things through if only she'd guarded her tongue?

"I don't know." She shoved the newspaper from the table to the floor. "I just don't know." She stood and went outside, her thoughts tumbling.

Ethan was entering a crucial time of his life. This fall, he'd be a senior in high school. He planned to go away to college next year. He'd been working so hard, saving as much as he could. He needed his father. He needed guidance.

"Where are you, Steven?"

She didn't understand how he could desert them this way. Was what she'd done so terrible it deserved abandonment? Did their years together, did their son, count for nothing at all?

I'm afraid, God. I'm terrified. I feel alone. Where are You in all of this?

She looked around the yard. The grass needed mowing, and she'd allowed weeds to encroach on her flower beds. She and Steven had always cared for their home together. They'd shared the duties. They'd been a team. And now her life partner had walked out without so much as a backward glance.

I've asked for Your help, Father, but things keep getting worse. Why is that? Don't You hear me? Is my sin so unforgivable?

She dashed tears from her cheeks with the backs of her hands.

Why are You punishing me this way? Was I wrong when I thought You spoke to me? Was I wrong to think things would work out?

Beloved . . . wait.

Erika caught her breath at the stirring in her heart.

Don't you know that the Lord is the everlasting God, the

Creator of all the earth? No one can measure the depths of His understanding.

God understood. He wasn't punishing her. The Lord understood her heart's cry.

Those who wait on the Lord will find new strength. They will fly high on wings like eagles.

Waiting. It was the hardest thing of all to do.

And yet, in those words from Isaiah, she believed God had spoken another promise to her, a promise for her future, a promise about her marriage.

God understood. He had a plan. She couldn't see it, but she would do her best to believe it.

She would trust.

She would wait.

CHAPTER Thirty-One

STEVEN HADN'T MISSED the weekly Bible study in over a year. But he didn't go this Thursday morning. He didn't want to explain his current situation to the men of his church.

His current situation. Now wasn't that a polite turn of phrase to describe where he found himself?

He rolled over, feeling every lump and bump in the cheap mattress and remembering his mom's nighttime refrain when he was a kid: *"Sleep tight. Don't let the bedbugs bite."* He never imagined he'd be sleeping in a sleazy motel at his age, wondering if it might actually *have* bedbugs.

Muttering an oath of disgust, he sat up on the side of the bed. He ran a hand over his face, feeling the growth of stubble on his jaw. He hadn't shaved all week, and he knew he looked like a skid-row bum. Fitting, he supposed, given his current place of residence.

If he was at home . . .

He suddenly wondered if Erika wished she hadn't told him to leave. Told him to leave? Well, so she hadn't exactly *told* him to go, but she'd suggested it might be for the best. That made this her fault. Right?

You haven't even called her. She doesn't know where you are.

He wondered if she was worried about him. Was she lying awake nights, thinking about him? The same way Steven was lying awake, thinking about her?

Her words whispered in his memory: *"You don't want to touch me. You never kiss me or tell me you love me. You walk wide circles around me. Like I'm a leper or something."*

She didn't understand. Couldn't understand. She had no idea how many times in the past weeks he'd wanted to reach for her—even in the midst of his anger. He'd wanted to find comfort in her arms. But every time he'd been tempted, he'd thought of Erika and Dallas together, and he'd turned away.

He'd always turned away.

⁂

Nick Franklin shook Dallas's hand as the study group broke up. "We're glad you joined us. Don't know what happened to Steven. It isn't like him to miss."

Dallas didn't think it was his business to tell the pastor about Erika and Steven's problems, so he said nothing.

"We hope you'll be back next week," Nick went on.

"Don't worry. I will be." This time Dallas smiled and nodded before heading to his car.

Never in his wildest dreams would Dallas have imagined he'd enjoy a Bible study. When he thought of the derogatory names he'd called Christians in the past, he cringed in shame.

But that was the old Dallas who'd said those things, he reminded himself. He was different now. He felt new, too. It was a difficult thing to describe, this feeling of newness. He'd tried to tell Paula, but she'd rolled her eyes and given him one of *those* looks.

I guess if You can reach me, You can reach her.

Maybe God was already reaching her. Dallas couldn't believe how much better things had been between them since last Sunday. Ironic, wasn't it? That was the same day Steven walked out on Erika.

He frowned as he pointed the remote at his car and pressed the button. The horn honked its brief alert, and the driver's-side door unlocked.

What could he do to help his friends? he wondered. Half a dozen times yesterday afternoon he'd picked up his phone to call Erika. And half a dozen times he'd placed the phone back in its cradle, never making the call. After all, what could he say to her? He didn't have any words of wisdom to share.

༄

Erika flipped the fried egg in the skillet, then checked the bacon in the microwave.

"Morning, Mom."

She glanced over her shoulder at Ethan. "Well, good morning. You're up early. I thought you had today off."

"I do. Just couldn't sleep."

"Want some breakfast?"

"No thanks." Ethan moved toward the fridge while rubbing his face with both hands. "Is there any orange juice?"

"I think so."

He opened the refrigerator door. "Yup. There's a little left in the carton. Want any?"

She shook her head. "You can have it."

The phone rang, and she caught her breath. Was it Steven calling?

"I'll get it," Ethan said. He picked up the receiver. "Hello?"

As she pulled the frying pan off the burner, Erika wondered if Ethan had hoped it was his dad, too.

"Hi . . . yeah, it's kinda early. . . . Sure, she's here. Just a sec." He held the phone toward his mother. "It's Paula."

Erika's heart sank with disappointment as she reached to take it from him. "Hello."

"Erika, I just heard about Steven leaving. It's awful. Just awful."

She closed her eyes, feeling the disappointment turn to a knot in her stomach. She hated others knowing. She particularly hated Paula knowing.

"You must be terrified," Paula continued. "I mean, there you are with no job experience or anything and almost forty years old. Do you have any idea what you're going to do now?"

"I'm praying," she answered softly.

"Well," Paula said with a laugh, "that might bring you comfort, Erika, but it won't pay your mortgage. I can guarantee it."

Fear of the unknown lifted its ugly head.

"You know I'll help if I can."

What was Paula after? A promise that Erika wouldn't tell Dallas about Warren Carmichael? Or had Paula called to gloat?

Paula asked, "How are you holding up emotionally?"

"Fine," Erika lied, wishing she could end the call.

"You two were the last couple I expected this to happen to. Of course, I understand how Steven feels about you and Dallas. I was plenty devastated myself, thinking of the two of you having a child together, then keeping it a secret all these years."

Paula's words were meant to sting, and they did.

"Speaking of Kirsten," Paula said, "I'm going to meet her tomorrow night. She's coming to our place for supper. I was hoping you might bring her. It would make it more comfortable for everyone if you're there."

Comfortable for everyone except Erika. She didn't want to go out. She didn't want to socialize. She certainly didn't want to be pitied by Paula Hurst.

"Why don't you talk to Kirsten and let me know? I've got a call coming in on the other line." Paula hung up.

"What'd she want?" Ethan asked as Erika set down the phone.

"Kirsten's going to their house tomorrow. Paula wants me to come, too."

"Are you gonna go?"

"What do you think I should do?" She turned to look at him.

He shrugged and said nothing.

She had a sudden image of herself as the child. Ethan was trying to be strong for her, but he was only seventeen. Seventeen and hurting because his father had left without a word.

"I'm sorry, Ethan," she said.

He didn't ask what for.

"Don't hold this against your dad. He loves you. This is about him and me, not you. He didn't mean to hurt you by leaving."

He met her gaze. "Don't make excuses for him, Mom."

Hearing the anger in her son's voice, Erika wondered if things would ever be right in her family again. The Bible said that all things were possible with God, but did she believe it was true? It chilled her to the core to think that her husband and their son might end up with the same strained relationship as Erika and her own father.

I've never forgiven Dad.

She turned toward the window, staring outside but looking inward.

That's why I act like a scared, fretful child around him. I've never forgiven him for being who he is.

The simple truth stunned her. Why hadn't she seen it before now?

Trevor James had never been the father she'd wanted him to be, the father she'd needed him to be. He'd failed her. He'd made her feel she wasn't good enough. He hadn't loved her the way she'd so desperately needed to be loved, especially after her mother died.

Now it's time I forgive him. It's time I made my peace with him. It's way past time.

⁓

Several hours later, Erika pulled her car to the curb in front of her father's house and cut the engine.

Help me, Lord.

She reached for the handle, opened the car door, then got out. With slow but determined steps, she made her way up the walk and rang the bell. She had plenty of time to change her mind before her father answered, but she held her ground.

"Erika?" he said when he opened the door, a frown furrowing his forehead. "What're you doing here?"

"I need to talk to you, Dad."

"Got another mystery kid to tell me about?"

The words hurt, but she did her best not to show it. "No."

Trevor turned and walked away, leaving the door open so she could follow.

I can do this.

The air inside the house was still and warm. The curtains were drawn against the late-afternoon sunlight.

Her father sat in his La-Z-Boy. "Well, spit it out. What've you done now?"

"Oh, Dad," she said on a sigh. "I haven't *done* anything." She settled onto the sofa. "We need to talk about . . . about us."

"Us?"

"You and me. The way we are with each other."

"Good grief. This isn't going to be like on *Oprah*, is it? Bare our souls and all that other nonsense."

Erika clenched her hands into fists in her lap. "Maybe."

"Oh, save me," her father muttered.

She fought unwelcome tears. "Do you know how much that hurts, Dad, when you say things like that?"

"You're the one who came to see me. I didn't ask you."

"No. No, you didn't ask. You never do. You've never wanted to simply spend time with me. You've always adored Ethan, but what about your daughter?"

He glowered.

"Dad?" She leaned forward. "Do you love me?"

"Do I—?" He stopped cold, then snapped, "That's the dumbest thing you've ever asked me."

"And you didn't answer."

"Don't think I will either."

"Why am I such a disappointment to you?"

"For cryin' out loud, girl. Don't you have anything better to do with your time than to irritate your old man?"

Erika wiped away the tears she couldn't keep from falling. "After Mommy died, I felt so alone. I needed you to hold me and make me feel special, the way other dads did their kids. I wondered what was wrong with me that you couldn't love me like that. I thought I'd get over the hurt after I married Steven, but I didn't."

"I always took care of you. You had everything you needed." Her father sank deep into his chair. He reminded Erika of a cornered animal. "You never went without," he added.

"Yes, I did." She stood. "I went without *you*."

He didn't respond.

"There was one time—" she looked down at her hands—"after I became a Christian, that I asked God if He could hold me in His arms and let me really *feel* a father's love. And He did."

Trevor snorted. He crossed his arms and turned his head away from her.

That was when she saw her father as he really was—a prisoner of his own emotions—and she felt sorry for him. Unless God intervened, he wasn't going to change. She would need to accept him—love him, honor him, forgive him—exactly as he was.

"Okay, Dad," she said. "Just remember, I love you. I love you, and I forgive you."

Time seemed to stop as she spoke those words, and in the stillness of that dimly lit room, Erika felt her childhood hurts being excised from her heart by a divine hand.

CHAPTER THIRTY-TWO

AT NINE-FIFTY ON FRIDAY MORNING, Steven watched the red-and-white Chevy pull into the employee parking lot behind the hardware store. He got out of his car and strode in that direction. Ethan was halfway to the rear entrance before Steven called out to him.

"Ethan, wait!"

His son stopped and turned. He didn't look any too happy to see him.

"Can you spare me a few minutes?"

Ethan checked his watch. "I guess so."

"I've wanted to talk to you about . . . about what's happening." Steven moved a few steps closer.

His son arched an eyebrow. "Really?" The word dripped with sarcasm.

"Yes."

"As far as I know, the phones have been working at our house all week."

Steven took the verbal hit, waited a few moments, then softly said, "I guess I deserve that."

Ethan shoved his fingertips into his jean pockets. "I guess you do." He frowned as he took in Steven's appearance. "You look like something I'd hate to step in."

Steven flinched. "I haven't been sleeping too good."

"Who has?"

Steven tried to stay calm. "How's your mom doing?"

"As if you care."

"I do care." His voice rose a little, along with a sense of frustration. He'd expected Ethan to give him a chance to explain his side of things. "I do care," he repeated. "But with everything that's happened, it's . . . it's kind of confusing."

"No, it isn't." Ethan's eyes sparked with anger. "It's real simple. You're always saying how we're supposed to do the right thing. Well, anybody can see you're not doing it."

"Ethan, you don't understand what—"

"You're right. I don't understand." Ethan stepped forward. "All my life you've told me how much you love Mom. Then you walk out on her like this? That's not love. So she made a mistake when she was in high school. Is being an unwed mother the unforgivable sin? Would you disown me if I fathered a kid at seventeen?"

"Ethan, you and Cammi aren't—?"

His son made a noise of disgust as he turned toward

the store's back door. "You need to get right with God, Dad." He hurried inside without a backward glance.

Steven stood still, rooted to the ground.

"You need to get right with God, Dad." The words pierced his heart, an arrow to the center of a bull's-eye. *"You need to get right with God, Dad."*

His pride demanded his son's words be rejected. Who was the father here and who was the child? A boy shouldn't talk that way to his dad.

But he's right, that pesky small voice whispered. *You do need to get right with God.*

⌇

If Kirsten had come to her father's alone that Friday evening, she would have turned around and left the instant she saw the house. She'd known Dallas Hurst was successful. But she hadn't expected *this.*

As Erika turned her car into the driveway, Kirsten looked at her and said, "How long have they lived here?"

"About six years, I think. They had it built a few years after they were married. Paula designed it herself."

"Tell me about her."

Erika seemed to consider her words before replying. "She's younger than your father. Just thirty this year. Very attractive. Career driven. She worked her way up in her father's real estate business. Not selling. Developing. She and Dallas like to travel a lot. Since they don't have any children or pets, there isn't much that ties them down except for their respective businesses."

Kirsten looked toward the large house again. "How long have they been married?"

"Almost nine years."

The front door opened, and Dallas appeared.

Erika waved at him.

Kirsten held her breath, her nerves screeching.

"Relax, honey. It's going to be fine." Erika opened her car door and got out.

After a moment's hesitation, Kirsten did the same.

Dallas came down the curving walkway to meet them. Behind him, still standing in the doorway, partially hidden in shadows, was a woman.

Dallas's wife.

Kirsten's stepmother.

Now *that* had an ominous ring.

None of Kirsten's research about finding and reuniting with birth parents had prepared her for the complexities of all these relationships. There'd been plenty of warnings, of course, but none had seemed to apply to her. She'd grown up with no one other than her adoptive mother—no father, no siblings, no grandparents or aunts or uncles. She'd rarely given any thought to what an extended family might mean.

"Hi," Dallas said as he drew closer. "Glad you could both come. Did you bring your swimsuits?"

"Yes," Erika answered.

Dallas turned toward Kirsten. He gave her a brief but encouraging smile. "Come on. Paula's eager to meet you."

Kirsten hoped that was true.

Dallas cupped her elbow with his hand and gently

propelled her toward the house. She went all aflutter inside, whether because she was about to meet her step-mother or because her father was holding her arm, she couldn't be certain.

Paula Hurst stepped through the doorway. She was a tiny slip of a thing with short red hair, green eyes, and a smattering of freckles. At first glance, pixie cute. At second glance, sophisticated and shrewd.

Oh, man. She hates my guts.

Paula smiled and extended her hand. "Kirsten, it's a pleasure to meet you." Her voice was so sweet sugar wouldn't melt in her mouth.

The two women shook hands but not for long.

"Erika," Paula continued, "we're glad you came, too." She smiled at Dallas, then turned and led the way inside, tossing over her shoulder, "Sweetheart, why don't you give Kirsten a quick tour? I'm sure she's *dying* to see the house. Erika and I will wait by the pool."

The hair on the back of Kirsten's neck stood on end.

"Do you want to see the house now," her father asked, "or wait until after you take a swim?"

"Now, I guess."

"Great. Follow me."

Forty-five minutes later, after showing Kirsten every other room in the house, Dallas led the way into the home gym on the second floor. Kirsten didn't say anything as she strolled around the large, brightly lit room, her fingers sliding over the exercise equipment—several weight machines, a stationary bike, and a treadmill. The wall facing the river was all glass, affording an inspiring view.

"Paula and I both belong to private clubs," her father said. "She likes to work with a personal trainer, and I like to play racquetball. But it's nice to have this to use when we can't make it out."

"Yeah, it must be."

She didn't bother to tell him that her last apartment could have fit into this room. Better to keep that to herself. It would sound like sour grapes. And maybe that was what it was. It was hard not to compare this house and all it represented with the hand-to-mouth life she and her mom had while Kirsten was growing up.

"Well, that's the end of the tour," Dallas said. "Why don't you use the bathroom at the bottom of the stairs to change into your swimsuit? I'll meet you by the pool."

"Okay."

Dallas turned, opened the glass door, then looked over his shoulder. "I'm glad you're here, Kirsten. I hope you'll feel at home with us."

～

"You need to get right with God, Dad."

Steven sat in the upholstered chair with its coffee-stained fabric and sunken springs, staring at the worn shag carpet.

"You need to get right with God, Dad."

He opened the drawer in the bedside stand and pulled out the Bible he'd placed there upon his arrival. He set it in his lap, unopened, and looked at its cover.

In his years as a Christian, he'd read the Bible straight

through a couple of times and had participated in many different studies. He believed this book contained the inspired word of God and that God could and did use it to speak to believers. But, he realized, he didn't know the first thing about coming to the Word in a time of crisis.

Maybe because there hadn't been any real crises until now. Maybe because he'd never really been tested.

Not knowing what else to do, he set the book on its spine and let it fall open: Matthew, chapter 19.

He began to read at the top of the page.

Someone came to Jesus with this question: "Teacher, what good things must I do to have eternal life?"

"Why ask me about what is good?" Jesus replied. "Only God is good. But to answer your question, you can receive eternal life if you keep the commandments."

"Which ones?" the man asked.

And Jesus replied: "'Do not murder. Do not commit adultery. Do not steal. Do not testify falsely. Honor your father and mother. Love your neighbor as yourself.'"

"I've obeyed all these commandments," the young man replied. "What else must I do?"

Jesus told him, "If you want to be perfect, go and sell all you have and give the money to the poor, and you will have treasure in heaven. Then come, follow me." But when the young man heard this, he went sadly away because he had many possessions.

Steven stopped, then read the verses a second time. It didn't seem like a passage that had anything to do with his problems. And yet . . .

But when the young man heard this, he went sadly away. . . .

The young man in the story went sadly away because he had many possessions and didn't want to let go of them. But Steven didn't have lots of possessions. So why did he seem stuck on that line?

Would you go away sadly?

Steven closed his eyes. *I don't understand, Lord.*

Don't I see every sparrow fall? Don't I number the hairs on your head?

Yes. Of course. But . . .

Isn't My grace sufficient for you?

༄

Erika felt relieved when she saw Dallas come out of the house. The wait had been excruciating, primarily because all Paula had talked about was Steven and the gloomy future his leaving meant for Erika. Erika had escaped into the pool a couple of times, but that hadn't dissuaded Paula for long.

"Where's Kirsten?" Erika asked as Dallas drew near.

"She's changing into her suit."

Paula rose from her lounger, kissed her husband's cheek, then said, "I'd better check on things in the kitchen. Be right back."

Dallas sat on the vacated lounge chair. Glancing at Erika, he gave her a sheepish grin. "I can't believe how nervous I've been about tonight."

"Kirsten's nervous, too."

"I didn't know I'd care so much so quick. You know what I mean? What Kirsten thinks of me, if she'll like me, if she and Paula will get along."

Erika nodded in understanding.

"I never expected to feel like this about her."

Softly, she asked, "Like what, Dallas?"

"I don't know. Possessive, maybe. Proud to be her father." He chuckled and shook his head. "Dumb, huh?"

"No, not dumb. Normal."

Dallas stared into the distance. "Maybe I shouldn't say this, but it's like you gave me a gift. Who knows if Paula and I will have kids of our own? So Kirsten . . . well, she may be the only daughter I ever have." He looked at Erika. "I feel guilty for being happy about it. I mean, with what's happened between you and Steve, I don't—"

"That isn't your fault, Dallas. Steven made his own choice, the same way we did."

He reached out and took hold of her hand. "I'm sorry all the same. If there's something I can do, anything at all, you just need to ask."

Erika nodded.

Dallas released her hand. "Sometimes I'd like to hit Steve for hurting you this way."

"Sometimes I'd like you to hit him, too." She smiled sadly.

"You know, I made fun of the way you two were,

your religion and all, but I always admired your marriage. I always wanted to have mine be as strong, to be the same kind of husband to Paula as Steve was to you. This just doesn't make any sense to me, the way he's been acting."

"Me, either," she whispered, dangerously close to losing the battle against tears. So she stood, walked to the water's edge, and dived in before Dallas could say anything else.

She swam the length of the pool, her thoughts churning faster than her arms.

It isn't fair, what Steven's done, and I'm angry. I'm alone and I'm scared. Right now, I don't even know if I want him to come home.

She reached the opposite end of the pool and clung to the side as she weighed the truth of her thoughts. How was it possible to want Steven to return with every breath she took and not want him to return at the same time?

Forget Dallas hitting him. If Steven chose to return, maybe she'd hit him herself.

৵

Kirsten stared at herself in the bathroom mirror.

"I'm glad you're here, Kirsten. I hope you'll feel at home with us."

Her father's words had repeated in her mind since he'd spoken them. They made her almost giddy with joy. All her dreams—everything she'd hoped for—were coming true.

"I've got a dad," she told her reflection. "He likes me. He's glad I'm here."

Grinning, she grabbed her towel, then turned and opened the door.

Paula Hurst was waiting in the hall.

Kirsten felt her smile evaporate.

"That's right," Paula said softly. "Let's not bother to pretend."

"Paula, I—"

"Let's get something straight, you and I. There's no place for you here, no matter what Dallas tells you. So enjoy this day while you can. You're going to be old news soon enough."

Kirsten tilted her chin, pretending a calm she didn't feel.

Paula leaned closer. "I'm his wife, and I'm not about to have my way of life threatened by the likes of you. You don't stand a chance."

"I'm not threatening anything. All I want is to know my dad."

"He isn't your dad. He's just a guy who did something stupid when he was drunk. He'll forget you as soon as he tires of the novelty of the situation. You realize that, don't you?"

Kirsten's knees felt rubbery. She wanted to escape. She wanted to retreat into the bathroom and slam the door.

Paula smiled victoriously. "I think I've made my point. If you tell Dallas what I said, I'll deny it. I'll have him believing you're a liar in no time at all." She turned. "Don't underestimate me, Miss Lundquist. Don't ever underestimate me."

CHAPTER THIRTY-THREE

DALLAS AWAKENED early the next morning, early
enough that moonlight still filtered through the slats in
the mini-blinds, striping the floor and the bed.

He rolled onto his side to gaze upon his sleeping wife.

Things had gone well the previous evening. While
there had been a little tension between Paula and Kirsten,
he thought his wife had done her utmost to make his
daughter feel welcome. He was grateful for the effort.

And Kirsten? The way he felt about her continued
to surprise and amaze him. He was just beginning to
know her, but already he'd discovered he loved her. He
wanted to be a good father, belated though his attempts
might be.

*Would she have turned out half as well if I'd been around when
she was growing up?*

He would never know for sure, but he liked to think so. Of course, when he looked back over his life, he had plenty of regrets. Plenty of them. He'd do it a lot differently if he had it to do over again. He would have tried to do it God's way a whole lot sooner.

Paula sighed in her sleep, then rolled onto her side, facing him. She looked adorable with her hair all mussed and her face serene in sleep.

Dallas was tempted to awaken her with kisses, but he decided the more loving thing to do would be to let her sleep. He rolled over and got out of bed. He'd go for his run now, and maybe by the time he was back, she'd be awake.

An hour later, he reentered the bedroom, sweaty from his run. Paula was still sleeping, so he quietly closed the bathroom door and proceeded to take his shower.

It was when he was drying off that he discovered the blister on his right heel. He searched for some ointment and a Band-Aid, looking in all the usual places, but he came up empty. So he checked Paula's side of the bathroom, including her makeup drawer.

Funny, how that blister became more painful just because he couldn't find what he wanted. There had to be a Band-Aid *somewhere!*

He pulled a gold-and-silver pouch from the drawer and tossed it onto the counter, not noticing until it was too late that the zipper wasn't closed. Several small packets fell to the floor.

Irritated, he reached to pick them up, reading the prescription label out of habit more than curiosity.

Paula Hurst . . . Desogen . . . 28 tablets . . .

It took him a moment, but finally he realized that these were packets of birth control pills. Only Paula hadn't been on the pill for several years.

Dr. Ulster, Barbara . . .

Paula's gynecologist.

2 Refills Remaining . . . Date Filled: June 28 . . .

The date, just two weeks ago, flashed at him like a neon sign.

June 28 . . .

He stared at the year. It was this year. He wasn't wrong about that.

June 28 . . .

Something hard and cold, like the long blade of a hunting knife, twisted in his gut.

He glanced at the other two packets, still sealed shut. Same date, same prescription number. He opened the first packet, hoping . . .

There were ten pills missing.

He pictured Paula whispering that she wanted to have his baby, that she'd seen the doctor, had taken some tests, and been told there was no reason she couldn't get pregnant, that if they were patient . . .

He closed his eyes, at the same time closing his hand around the packet and squeezing hard, as if he could crush that plastic container and make the pills go away.

"Dallas, are you done in the—"

He spun toward the door. Paula was there, staring at him, wearing a horrified expression.

After several dreadful moments, she asked, "What were you doing in my things?"

"You've been on birth control. All this time. All this time while I was wondering if there was something wrong with me or with you. You've been taking the pill."

"It isn't what it looks like."

He could almost see the wheels turning in her head as she searched for an explanation. And he knew, whatever she came up with, it would be a lie.

"It was only for a while," she said. "To help my system regulate."

Dallas stepped toward her, took her hand, and pressed the packet onto her palm, then closed her fingers around it. "That isn't the truth, and we both know it." He walked by her, needing some distance.

"How dare you call me a liar!"

"How dare I?" He turned around. The ice in his belly turned to fire. "How *dare* I?"

"You had no right getting into my things. I would've told you when the time was right."

"It still would've been a lie."

She threw the packet at him. Her aim was true. It struck him on the chest, above his heart. Next, she hurled a vile name in his direction. That one hit its mark, too.

He felt anger. He felt anguish. He felt like somebody's fool. He turned and strode away a second time.

Paula followed him through the bedroom and out into the hall. "Don't you walk away, Dallas Hurst. Don't you act all high-and-mighty. You're no saint, and I don't care how much religion you get. You're no better than me."

He kept walking.

She kept following.

"I'll take you to the cleaners in a divorce," she shouted. "Remember that. I'll hire a private detective and find out about *your* affairs. See how lily white you are."

That, at last, stopped his forward motion. He turned slowly to face her. He stared hard into her eyes. "I've never cheated on you, Paula. Maybe I was tempted, but I never did. No private detective's going to find otherwise. Search all you want."

Something awful flickered across her beautiful face, something she hadn't meant for him to see.

That was when he understood another ugly truth.

He *was* somebody's fool.

Paula's.

&

When Kirsten spoke with her mother that morning, she didn't repeat what Paula Hurst had said, partly because she didn't want her mother to worry, partly because she didn't want to think about it herself. So she talked at length about her father's beautiful home and how nice he'd been to her and what a delicious supper they'd had.

When Kirsten finally paused, Donna said, "I'm glad for your sake that it's turning out so well. I was worried you'd get your hopes up, only to get hurt. I know how much you've longed to have a father in your life. Sometimes that hunger in your eyes liked to have broke my heart."

"You knew?"

"Oh, baby. Of course I knew. Every girl wants a

daddy who'll treat her like a little princess. If he'd lived, Felix would have done exactly that. You would've been spoiled rotten, no doubt about it. He loved you so much." There was a tiny catch in her voice. "You never saw a man as happy as he was the day we got you. When you were two, you used to run to the door when he'd get home from work, your chubby little legs going as fast as they could. You'd throw yourself at him, and he'd love all over you, hugging and kissing and tickling and laughing."

Kirsten wished she could remember it.

"But I'm glad you've found someone to . . . to fill his empty shoes. I hope with all my heart that this Dallas Hurst will love you and cherish you the way your . . . the way Felix did."

Kirsten could tell her mother was fixing to have a good cry. "Mom—"

"Honey, I've gotta run." Sniff. "Always lots to do on a Saturday." Sniff. "You call again soon, okay?"

"I will. I promise. Bye, Mom."

"Bye-bye."

After hanging up, Kirsten lay on the sofa, covered her eyes with her right forearm, and imagined herself as a toddler, throwing herself into Dallas's welcoming embrace.

Harvest Fellowship had a small prayer chapel at the back of the building that was open twenty-four hours a day. It was simply furnished—two short pews; a prayer altar; a plain wooden cross before a round stained-glass window, track lighting turned low.

Steven sat in the front pew, Bible open on his lap.

Sometime in the night, when he lay sleepless on that lumpy motel mattress staring at the ceiling, he'd begun to wonder why he'd never been truly tested in his Christian walk. He wondered what that said about him and his faith. Finally, he'd opened his Bible and began looking for answers.

He recalled different passages now:

"He will sit and judge like a refiner of silver, watching closely as the dross is burned away."

"These trials are only to test your faith, to show that it is strong and pure. It is being tested as fire tests and purifies gold—and your faith is far more precious to God than mere gold."

"For when your faith is tested, your endurance has a chance to grow. So let it grow, for when your endurance is fully developed, you will be strong in character and ready for anything."

"I proved weak in character," Steven whispered. "I wasn't ready for anything. I failed the test. I failed my family." His chest ached. "I failed You, Lord. Forgive me."

"If we confess our sins to him, he is faithful and just to forgive us and to cleanse us from every wrong."

It was amazingly easy to get God's forgiveness, Steven thought. All he needed to do was confess and repent, and he'd be forgiven and cleansed. God's grace and mercy were boundless. He would set Steven's sins as far from him as the east is from the west.

I guess that's the problem. How easy it is, how great is Your mercy.

He hadn't understood what grace meant. Not really. If he had, he wouldn't have taken it for granted. He wouldn't have been such a jerk, sitting on his high horse and judging those around him. Judging Erika especially.

She's right. I have been self-righteous. Father, forgive me.

He knew that God's forgiveness was his the moment he asked, but it would be much harder to gain forgiveness from those here on earth whom he'd hurt with his words and his actions.

How do I begin? How do I win their forgiveness and earn back their trust?

He thought of Kirsten, thought of the way he'd reacted to her from the first moment he'd learned of her. He'd hated her. There, that was the truth. He'd hated her for living, even more so when he'd seen how much she looked like Erika and Dallas.

But Kirsten was loved by God. Her life had value to the Lord. God had formed her in Erika's womb. How had Steven dared to despise her when God loved her? Wasn't his wishing she'd never been born the same as wishing her aborted?

O Father, forgive me. I didn't understand.

He heard the soft squeak of the chapel door opening. He hoped it wasn't someone he knew. Most of all he hoped it wasn't Pastor Tischler or Pastor Nick. He wasn't ready to talk. Not while he was trying to wrap his understanding around it all.

He heard entering footsteps, then a pause, then the footsteps again. He supposed he'd have to look up to see who was there.

"Steve."

He turned toward the aisle, his gaze colliding with Dallas's.

"Sorry to intrude," his friend said. "If you want—" he jerked his head toward the door—"I can leave."

Steven wanted to reply in the affirmative. Then he remembered the prayer he'd lifted moments before: *How do I begin?* It seemed God's answer had come quickly. "No," he said. "You don't need to leave." He slid to his right on the pew. "Go ahead and sit down."

Dallas sat.

Both men turned their eyes toward the cross and waited, the silence of the chapel closing around them. Dust particles drifted through the air, colored by the light filtering through the stained-glass window.

After a long while, Steven said, "I never thought of myself as a jealous man, but I've discovered I am. I thought of Erika as mine, as my very own possession. But she isn't mine. She's God's, and she has a right to make mistakes, just like anybody else." He glanced toward Dallas. "And so do you."

Dallas rubbed a hand over his face before saying, "I've made plenty of them."

Steven thought he looked defeated. That wasn't normal. His friend usually wore an air of cocky self-confidence.

"Are you going home now?" Dallas asked.

"I don't know." Steven turned once again toward the cross, feeling the shame for what he'd done, what he'd put his family through. "I don't know if Erika or Ethan will want me to."

"They will. They do."

"I hope you're right."

More silence. More reflection.

Again it was Steven who broke the stillness. "I never even rejoiced over your salvation. I prayed for it for years, and then I wasn't glad when it happened because of my jealousy and anger." *O God, how did I sink so low?* "I'm sorry, Dallas. I'm real sorry."

"It's okay."

Pride, Steven believed, was at the root of all sin, and pride was a hard thing to swallow. "Will you forgive me for the things I've said and done the last few weeks?"

Dallas seemed to understand the importance of the moment. He didn't reply quickly or in an easy, offhanded manner. He met Steven's gaze with a serious one of his own, and only after a long while did he answer. "I forgive you, Steve. You're more than my best friend. You're my brother in Christ."

As they embraced, Steven knew this would be the easiest of the reconciliations. Nonetheless, he was glad to have it behind him.

When they broke apart, Steven asked, "So how'd you know to find me here?"

"I didn't know. I . . . I needed a place to pray." He swallowed hard, then said, "Paula's been having an affair. I found out this morning. I should have figured it out before this, but I guess I had blinders on."

"Oh, man."

Dallas released a humorless laugh. "Oh, man."

Here we are. Both of us with marriages on the rocks.

As if reading Steven's thoughts, Dallas said, "The difference between us is, your wife loves you. Paula made it pretty clear before she left the house this morning that any love she once felt for me died long ago."

Steven wanted to tell his friend that things would work out, but platitudes wouldn't cut it. So he slipped an arm around Dallas's shoulders, and the two of them sat in silence.

CHAPTER THIRTY-FOUR

STEVEN SAT ON THE FRONT STOOP, waiting for Erika to return home. He had a key, but he wouldn't use it. He had no right to use it until she told him he could.

If she told him he could.

He was scared. Scared things wouldn't work out the way he wanted.

Erika's car pulled into the driveway, and Steven rose from the step, waiting, his heart pumping. When she got out, she stared at him, her face an expressionless mask. He couldn't tell if she was happy or horrified to see him.

She closed the car door and walked slowly in his direction.

"Did I come at a bad time?" he asked as she drew near.

She shook her head.

"I hoped we could talk."

"You look tired, Steven."

"I haven't slept well." He could have told her she looked tired, too. He didn't.

"You cut yourself shaving," she said, pointing at the nick on his jaw.

"I was out of practice." He shrugged, then shook his head before she could ask him what he meant. "Can we talk?"

With a nod, she unlocked the door and led the way inside.

Steven would have preferred to hold this discussion in the kitchen, but Erika went into the living room. She sat on the sofa. He took the chair opposite her. Her posture was rigid, her hands folded in her lap. She looked fragile. She'd lost weight. There were dark smudges beneath her eyes.

I did this to her.

Something inside him broke under the load of guilt.

⁓

Erika ached at the sight of him, at the distance between them. If only Steven would get out of that chair and come sit beside her. If only he would take her in his arms and hold her the way he used to, the way that had always made her feel cherished and safe.

But even as she longed for those things, she wondered what she would do if he tried. She wondered if she would let him. There was so much hurt in her heart.

Do I even still love him?

How quickly she could have answered that question in the past. But today? Today she felt only emptiness where the love had once been.

"Why did you come, Steven?" she asked at last.

"I need to ask for your forgiveness."

Forgive him? He'd been gone nearly a week without a word, without so much as a telephone call to tell her where he was staying, and now he wanted her to forgive him. Was that all he had to say?

"I . . . ah . . ." He paused to clear his throat. "I went to see Ethan at work yesterday. Did he tell you?"

Erika shook her head.

"He said I needed to get right with God."

She could imagine the way Ethan had said it, too. She almost smiled.

"He was right," Steven said softly. "That's what I needed. I was angry at you, so I got angry at God, and then I ran away from Him . . . and you."

A week ago, his simple confession would have been enough for Erika. A week ago, she would have made it easy on him.

This wasn't a week ago.

༄

Steven couldn't sit still any longer. He felt pierced by Erika's unwavering, unrelenting gaze. He rose and paced to the window, where he stared out at the lengthy after-noon shadows.

"You were always so perfect in my eyes," he said

after a while. "That was the problem, I guess. I imagined that you were perfect, and then I expected you to be exactly what I imagined. I expected you to never make a mistake—past, present, or future. I put you up on some fancy pedestal and expected you to stay where no human being *can* stay for long." He glanced over his shoulder. "When you fell off, I blamed you rather than myself."

She continued to meet his words with silence, and he had no clue whether or not he was getting through.

You could have told me about Kirsten, he was tempted to say, the impulse to justify his actions springing suddenly back to life. He pushed the urge away as he turned toward her.

"Last night, God showed me that when I'm discontent with my life, the life He gave me, then I'm arguing with Him. I'm saying He isn't sufficient, He isn't enough. I'm saying that what I want is more important or better than what He wants for me."

She sat so still, he wondered if she listened or heard.

"When I walked out of here, I was like the rich young man in the Bible. I didn't want to give up what I thought was rightfully mine."

"What was that?" she asked.

"A perfect you."

She gave her head a slow shake.

"You were right, Erika. I *was* self-righteous. I realize it now. I had no concept of God's grace, of what it really is. I just accepted it as if it were my due instead of a gift." He hesitated a moment, then asked, "Are you able to forgive me?"

She looked at him with that unemotional gaze and whispered, "Am I able?"

He had the distinct impression she was asking the question of herself rather than echoing him. He held his breath, waiting for the answer.

Am I able to forgive you? I don't know. Even if I knew, I'd be afraid to say it. What if we fail each other again? What if the next time we're with Kirsten or Dallas you remember what I did and you hold it against me? What if you resent having Kirsten as a part of our lives? Because if she's part of mine, she's part of yours, like it or not.

Gently, in the midst of her stormy thoughts, she felt God's touch upon her heart.

I'll guide you, beloved. Trust me.

I'll try, Lord.

"Erika?"

She nodded. "Yes, I think I can forgive you."

He took a step toward her.

She put out a hand, like a traffic cop, knowing there was more that had to be said. "It isn't that simple."

He stopped, and his shoulders slumped.

"If you put me on a pedestal, Steven, then I suppose I did the same to you. You were my high school sweetheart, my first and only love. I thought the sun and moon rose and set with you." She drew a shuddery breath, feeling her way, thinking aloud, facing things she'd never truly faced before. "Perhaps I made idols of you and our marriage, setting you higher than the Lord." She sighed deeply. "It would be easy to pretend that none of this happened, to pretend we didn't hurt each other the way we have."

"But you didn't—"

"Don't. Don't say I didn't hurt you. I did, and we must be free to talk about everything if we're going to tear down the wall between us." She stood. "What I'm trying to say is, we can't simply go back to the way things were, as if none of this happened. We'll have to work on our marriage and find ways to make it what it should be, what God intended it to be, not what we imagined it was."

"That's what I want, too."

"Will you go with me to counseling?"

He nodded, looking both shaken and hopeful. "Yes."

"And you'll be at church tomorrow?"

Steven heard the question and understood. She was saying she didn't want him to come home yet. He was disappointed, but he couldn't blame her.

"Yes," he answered, "I'll be there."

She turned and led the way into the hall. At the front door she gave him the slightest of smiles and said, "Ethan and I will watch for you there."

When was the last time he'd held his wife in his arms? When was the last time he'd kissed her mouth or touched her shoulder or held her hand? Weeks. Eons. It seemed forever. He wished he could do it now, but he couldn't. He had given up that right of his own accord, and now he would have to earn it back.

He walked past her, opened the front door, and stepped onto the stoop. Then he paused and turned toward her. "Do you think you'll be able to love me again someday?"

"Someday?" Now there were tears in her eyes. "Steven, because you're my husband, I choose to love you today."

He nodded. She *chose* to love him. It wasn't what he'd wanted her to say. He'd wanted to see the love in her eyes, to hear it in her voice. But a decision to love him was what he'd received.

For now, that would have to be enough.

Chapter Thirty-Five

KIRSTEN KNEW SHE'D SUFFERED a weak moment. Otherwise, she wouldn't be standing outside her apartment on a Sunday morning—wearing a dress, for crying out loud!—waiting for her father to take her to church.

But how could she deny his invitation, especially after she learned that Paula had left him.

I'm like a marriage torpedo, she thought with chagrin.

Still, when she remembered the things Paula had said to her on Friday, she couldn't help feeling a small thrill of victory, too. She supposed that wasn't entirely a good way to feel, but there it was.

Her father's Lexus rounded the corner and pulled to the curb in front of her.

Dallas smiled. "Morning."

"Good morning."

"Are you ready?"

As ready as I'll ever be, she thought. She opened the car door and got in.

"Thanks for agreeing to come."

"I'm not exactly the churchgoing type, but I don't suppose it'll kill me."

Her father laughed. "I guarantee it won't. And up until a couple weeks ago, I thought the same way as you."

"Really?"

"Really." Dallas put the car in gear, then drove through the complex toward the road. As he pulled into the light Sunday morning traffic, he said, "I've got a favor to ask."

"What?"

"I'd like to introduce you as my daughter." He glanced at her, then back at the road. "Is that all right with you?"

Was it all right? All *right?* It was what she'd hoped for, dreamed of, but never expected to really happen.

"And if you ever feel you can," Dallas added, "I'd like you to call me Dad. I know it's too soon now. You hardly know me. But someday, when you feel you can."

Someday, Kirsten thought with joy. *Someday.*

Knowing she would see Steven in church made Erika as nervous as a teenager on prom night.

Lord, don't allow me to rush ahead of You.

Wait, the Lord had told her. Trust Him, for He held

her in the palm of His hand. Lean on Him, for He was her rock and her fortress.

Help me to listen and be patient. Help me to see You at work when it seems nothing is happening.

Wait, for God alone was the restorer. He made new things out of old. He would make something new out of her marriage. She believed it this morning with every fiber of her being.

Father, don't let me ever again make an idol of my marriage or of my husband. Don't let Steven put me back on a pedestal.

Erika's prayers continued as she and Ethan drove to church, as they made their way to their usual pew, as they greeted friends around them. As difficult as it was, she didn't allow herself to turn every ten seconds toward the sanctuary door. She waited at least thirty seconds between turns.

She felt a rush of pleasure when she saw Dallas's and Kirsten's arrival. She hadn't known Kirsten would be with him.

Father and daughter sat in the pew directly behind Erika and Ethan. Erika smiled at Kirsten, then met Dallas's gaze, their exchange silent but understood: Yes, they would both pray for Kirsten to know the Lord.

She glanced toward the entrance again, and this time, there was Steven, walking with purpose down the center aisle. His stride shortened when he noticed who sat behind Erika. He stopped to greet Dallas, then took hold of Kirsten's hand and leaned forward until his mouth was near her ear. Erika had no clue what he whispered, but she saw first the surprise on Kirsten's face and then her relief.

Another new beginning.

It won't be easy, Jesus. We're all still finding our way. Me, Steven, Ethan, Dallas, Kirsten. Maybe even Paula. Steven and I have hurt each other, and old hurts have a way of rising up unexpectedly. But we've made a good start, he and I, and I'll never let go of Your promises again. I'll trust You, no matter what.

Steven looked at Erika. She saw the hope in his eyes, as well as the uncertainty, the guilt, the pain. She saw the eyes of the father of her son, the eyes of her husband. They were the eyes that had looked tenderly into hers on their wedding night, the eyes that had watched her when she gave birth to Ethan, the eyes that had sparkled with laughter and glittered with tears through all the ups and downs of their lives.

We'll make it because greater is He that is in us than he that is in the world.

Steven stepped into the aisle, then toward Erika's pew. He held her gaze a long while before looking at their son. Steven held out his hand toward Ethan. The boy stood.

Softly, Steven said, "You were right, Son. I had to get right with God."

Ethan took the proffered hand.

Two men—one in midlife, one with a lifetime before him—both with good hearts. Cut from the same cloth, these two, father and son.

At long last, Steven sat beside Erika. But not too close. He kept his distance from her as he looked toward the front of the sanctuary, where the worship team was now assembling, his expression thoughtful.

For a moment, Erika's joy dimmed. Her hope faded. For a moment more, she doubted, the distance between them feeling too vast to be crossed.

Had she heard wrong? Had what she thought was a promise been only what she wanted and not what God had spoken?

Then her husband did something both simple and miraculous.

He reached out and took hold of her hand, his grasp gentle but sure. A grasp that said, *I won't let go again.*

He looked at her. She looked at him.

And once more, for today and for all of her tomorrows, Erika chose to love.

A Note from the Author

Dear Reader:

Many years ago, someone said to me, "You shouldn't have to work at marriage. If you're in love, it should be easy." That's a lie, but one that countless men and women in our culture have bought into. Marriages will never be perfect because people aren't perfect. We are flawed, and no matter how hard we try not to, we will fail the people we love.

I started to fall in love with my husband, Jerry, the day we met. He was thirty-four at the time, and when I asked him if he'd ever been married, he answered, "No. I've always believed marriage should be for a lifetime, and I haven't found the woman I want to spend the rest of my life with yet." I remember thinking, *Commitment! What a concept!*

I was gone—hook, line, and sinker.

Has our marriage been perfect? Far from it. We have traveled through dark and dangerous valleys, my husband and I, but we've come out on the other side as a couple, with God's help. We've come out because, like Erika, we *choose* to love one another. And perhaps we choose to love because we have begun to grasp, like Steven, a fuller meaning of God's grace.

May you be aware of God's grace in your life and in your marriage today.

In His grip,
Robin Lee Hatcher

About the Author

Author Robin Lee Hatcher, winner of the Christy Award for Excellence in Christian Fiction and the RITA Award for Best Inspirational Romance, has written over thirty-five contemporary and historical novels and novellas. There are more than 5 million copies of her novels in print, and she has been published in fourteen countries. Her first hardcover release, *The Forgiving Hour*, was optioned for film in 1999. Robin is a past president/CEO of Romance Writers of America, a professional writers organization with over eight thousand members world-wide. In recognition of her efforts on behalf of literacy, Laubach Literacy International named the Robin Award in her honor.

Robin and her husband, Jerry, live in Boise, Idaho, where they are active in their church and Robin leads a women's Bible study. Thanks to two grown daughters, Robin is now a grandmother of four ("an extremely young grandmother," she hastens to add). She enjoys travel, the theater, golf, and relaxing in the beautiful Idaho mountains. She and Jerry share their home with Delilah the Persian cat, Tiko the Shetland sheepdog, and Misty the Border collie.

Readers may write to her at P.O. Box 4722, Boise, ID 83711-4722 or visit her Web site at www.robinleehatcher.com.

ROBIN LEE HATCHER

From her heart . . . to yours

RIBBON OF YEARS

hardcover ISBN 0-8423-4009-2

Standing at the edge of her dreams, Miriam passionately embraces the future. Through tears and joy her ordinary life becomes a remarkable journey as she impacts others in miraculous ways.

"This poignant view of one woman's life is a superb read, and one I am glad I did not miss!"—**Romance Reader's Connection**

"Keep tissues handy. Miriam's life isn't sugarcoated, but a testament to triumph over adversity."—**CBA Marketplace**

*f*IRSTBORN

hardcover ISBN 0-8423-4010-6 · softcover ISBN 0-8423-5557-X

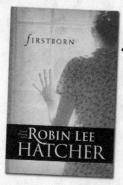

Erika's worst fear is realized when her well-kept secret shows up on her doorstep. As she reaches out to the daughter she gave up for adoption nearly twenty-two years ago, her husband pulls away, leaving Erika with an impossible choice.

"This is a well-written inspirational novel."
—**Publishers Weekly**

"Robin is a gifted writer whose novels unfailingly stir and challenge readers' hearts."—**Francine Rivers**

Turn the page for an exciting preview from *New Wine: A Love Story* by Robin Lee Hatcher (ISBN 0-8423-4011-4).

Available Fall 2003 from Tyndale House Publishers.

MARCH 19, 1955 MERIDIAN, IDAHO

THE FIRST TIME I saw Daniel Clermont—although I wouldn't know his name until later—was at Andy's funeral.

It was after the pastor said his last prayer, words meant to comfort me, Andy's widow. It was after friends and folks from church came and whispered their condolences as they touched my hands, kept folded tightly in my lap. It was after Andy's father— his face stoic, as hard as stone—led his weeping wife away, and I thought myself alone in that row of gray folding chairs at the graveside, the cold March wind buffeting my back.

It was after all that when I noticed him, standing under a leafless tree, staring at the casket before it was lowered into the grave. The collar of his overcoat was turned up, and he gripped the brim of his hat with one hand, lest it be blown away. I knew he wasn't one of those soft-spoken, grim-faced men from the funeral home, nor did he look like a groundskeeper. He was here because of Andy, I knew without a doubt, but he was a stranger to me.

He saw me watching him then. Removing his hat, he approached. "Mrs. Haskin," he said as he stopped before me, "I'm sorry for your loss, ma'am."

"Thank you," I whispered, the words like sandpaper in my throat. Meaningless words, really, in a mind gone numb with pain and dread and fear.

"Andy was a good man."

"Yes," I managed to say.

"If there's anything I can do, anything you need, anything at all . . ." His sentence drifted into silence, unfinished.

I nodded, wanting him to go away, wanting everyone to leave me alone. What I needed was to die and go to heaven with Andy. It wasn't right that I should be left behind. Andy and I were supposed to grow old together. Andy was supposed to build a new barn this summer, and I was supposed to plant roses along the white picket fence near the road. Andy was supposed to have sons to help him on our little farm, and I was supposed to have daughters to sew pretty dresses for.

I stared down at my hands. Black gloves against a black skirt. Black like my heart. Black and empty and bottomless.

Oh, Andy. Andy. Why did you have to die? What will I do without you?

When I looked up again, the stranger was gone.

"Come home, Phoebe," my mother said, more times than I could count, in the days that followed the funeral. "You can live with us. Dad and I want you here. You know we do. You shouldn't be alone now."

But how could I leave the farm? How could I let go of Andy's dream? It was all I had left of him, these forty acres and the house and outbuildings that sat on them. Strange, I suppose, that I wanted to stay, given it was the farm that took Andy from me. And yet, it was where I felt closest to him. He'd loved the land so. He'd loved being a farmer.

It was on a day when I pondered those very thoughts again, feeling despair welling up in me, that Daniel appeared at my door. I didn't recognize him at first. I was expecting a neighbor or someone from church with another casserole or a ham or more fried chicken. Every day since the funeral someone had brought something. Most of it was going to waste. I had no appetite.

"Mrs. Haskin," he said from beyond the screen door, hat in hand, his black hair whipped by a bitter wind.

"Yes?"

"I'm Daniel Clermont. I spoke to you at . . . at the cemetery last week."

"Oh." I made no attempt to make him feel welcome. "Yes. I remember."

"Andy and I served together in Korea."

Korea. Fear had been my constant companion when

Andy was in the army. But he'd survived. Survived and come home to me, whole and happy. Two years. We'd only had two years of bliss.

I placed my hand on the doorjamb, supporting legs suddenly gone weak.

"He saved my life," Daniel added softly.

Mine, too. Oh, Andy. Mine, too.